Hunted Season 1 Episode 1

S. H. Miah

Muslim Fiction Project

Contents

Disclaimer

I ask readers to understand that, in telling any story of mine, a main character may do un-islamic or prohibited things due to their flaws or ignorance. I assure that there is a positive character arc at play in all my stories, and ask of you to remain patient and see it through.

Jazakallahu Khairan for reading.

1

My prison cell is filled with fizzing. Electricity fizzing, if I want to give some more detail. And that electricity crackles like it wants to fry my entire body, and then eat me alive like a bear on the hunt.

Oh, what I would do for a bear. I'd skin it with my own hands, then rip its flesh out. I don't even know how I'd get a fire brewing. Maybe break apart a few twigs in some forest somewhere, then strike them together.

Then in the bear entrails would go. I'd cook that up, slice and dice with a shiv, then guzzle it as the best meal I'd have in years. And I don't even know what the heck a bear tastes like. And I've forgotten the taste of every other kind of meat I had before being chucked in this place.

Instead of freedom, I'm stuck here in the Enclave Prison. The Enclave wants to keep me here, on suspicion of some kind of terrorist charge. No evidence, no trial like they claim, no sense of justice. Just whoever they suspect gets the slammer, as my father used to say.

The only charge I can see in this prison is the electricity, and it seems to be getting closer as I lie in the makeshift bed, dunked onto the grey, metallic floor, a bed made from rags thinner than my skin at this moment.

If I wanna get some comfort, I'll have to finally get some sleep, since the real world offers no peace. My cell is about three by five, infinitely grey all over like a void of ambivalence, with only me inside. That's all the company I got, other than the two guards that come in to give the daily meals. And, of course, the hour of closely watched social time a week so we don't mentally go insane.

The guards wear large helmets, carry batons with a higher voltage than the electric bars of my cell, and their eyes are dark, hooded, hidden beneath the red mask they all have to wear as part of the Enclave's ensemble.

I don't know the next man that comes to my cell, and the guards don't know each other, either. All a part of the secrecy act they must abide by. That's as far as I know.

We're the worst of the worst, apparently. The ones that have to be kept inside for their own safety, as well as the safety of others. Not because we did anything to be here, but because of what we could do when we get out.

We're dangerous, and maybe that's the only source of strength I can find in here. That a government with the vice-like hold of the Enclave fears someone like me.

It's good to be feared. It can help you get your way with others. And the Enclave has most of Old Britain in a chokehold they can't escape, at least from the stirrings of gossip I hear during social time whispers.

The bloody lights are on again outside, blaring into the cell as if trying to fry my retinas the same way the electric charges want to. Someone needs to turn the damn things off to let me get some sleep. But no, there's a curfew around here, and it doesn't care that some of the inmates just want some shut eye without the bloody incisions of light.

I roll over to my side, ignoring the hurt bundling in through a shoulder, then down to my stomach. There is no pillow to cushion my head, just metal flooring with as much comfort as a smack with a baton.

My eyes flit to the other end of the cell, where a basin sits behind a little bit of chipped wall that blocks the guards from viewing my genitalia whenever I take a piss.

I glance a little to the left of that, the smell of my own piss from earlier drifting into my nose. It makes me gag, and I clamp down on the impulse to retch fully. The toilet flushes every three days, and today's the third since the last flushing.

There's a security camera in the top left corner of the cell, wide angle, with a look into every nook and cranny of the room. From what I've been told—which is barely anything but the little chatter from the hour of social time I get every week—those cameras have the ability to fire electric shocks.

Meaning if the Enclave so much as suspect me getting out of line for even a second, I'm done for. Done for and dead. Before I could even live at all.

A bit of a sorry life for Mason Sharp, prison extraordinaire. Maybe they'll write a book about me. A book about the man who was locked up when he was still a teenager for the crimes of his father when the Uprising failed.

And now Mason Sharp sits in his cell, wondering how the world could have went so wrong. How the Enclave could've taken everything away in the space of a sun's heartbeat.

I sigh, roll back over to the other side, let my breath mist the air as the temperatures drop for the night. I hear a crackle, the charges of the cell bars intensifying in case I get the idea to escape. My eyes close, the black and red void pulsing with a warm welcome, away from the chills of reality.

I remember when I was a child, when education was still allowed for citizens, I read something about cold temperatures allowing for better sleep, so the body could rest easier without the stifling heat.

Well, the Enclave takes that to the extreme. They installed these little vents in each cell that suck out the heat from everywhere in the cell with a sickening hiss, and then fill it with a snake-like chill. A chill that slithers its way over the cell like a wolf on the hunt, before finding the inmate and ensnaring him with a biting cold that won't let go till the morning comes.

I hear a rattle in the distance. The doors are locked for the night, all throughout the prison. Then, the few spots of redness in my eyelids vanish. Then, the world dims, giving way to another night of fitful sleep that I don't wish to wake from.

The next time my eyes open, I expect the typically blaring light that signals morning and slave labour. But instead of that, I feel a shock to my shoulder, a dull shock. Immediately my body tenses. I've been electrically charged, and the pain slowly diffuses to the rest of my body.

Wait, electric charges aren't slow. They're the fastest weapons the Enclave have. Deadly fast, fizzing through flesh at close to the speed of light and faster than the speed of sound, with the ability to debilitate the victim for easy detainment.

That's the way they'd caught me, after all. Shock and detain is the Enclave's game.

I glance around the cell without moving a single muscle. A shiver races over my spine from the immense cold, and I clamp my jaws to stop my teeth from chattering. Meaning it's still night time. The snake-like cold still slithers as ominously as ever.

The shock originated from my shoulder, the shoulder that faced the prison bars, with the other shoulder dug into the prickling mattress. My eyes shift, ever so slightly, to the cell bars. Nothing lies beyond that, except the infinite blackness I've come to sympathise with.

My hand then moves, snakes over to my shoulder and feels around. Shocks don't happen for no reason, after all. They're induced, one way or another.

And that's when I feel it. Digging into my shoulder is something sharp, at least on the first touch. And sharp things, more than anything else, shouldn't be in here.

Sweat lines the top of my forehead as my body temperature battles the artificial cold. I roll over, since the item is on my left shoulder which faces the ceiling. The item drops right in front of me, thumping the mattress, and it takes everything in my body not to gasp.

Somebody must be trying to frame me. Somebody must be trying to get me in trouble with the Enclave. Those bloody cameras have night vision, meaning there's not a place for me to hide.

I sneak my hand out again and grip the object jutting into the skin-thin mattress I sleep on. It's sharp at one edge, clearly, and made from something almost as cold as the air flowing in through the ventilation system.

I let my hand travel along the sharp edge, and realise there's something a lot more solid at the other end. As my hand roves over the object—it's a hilt.

The other side of the object is a hilt.

Which means, for whatever reason unfathomable to me, I've been sent a knife. A weapon. Something that would get me killed by the Enclave in a heartbeat.

I look through the darkness, into the corners of the black murk. I recall being a young boy again, and being scared of the dark. I didn't want to sleep due to the fear, but my father would sit down with me on the edges of my crooked wooden bed, let my gaze wander the darkness of my spindly bedroom, and reassure me there were no Enclave monsters ready to attack me.

His words don't apply here, though. Whoever sent me the weapon knows the implications. Knows that I could be executed in a heartbeat if the guards see even a glimpse of it.

I don't know why the Enclave are keeping me alive after killing my father, murdering him outright. I always thought the Enclave would kill me, too. Let me follow in his footsteps right till the end.

But they didn't, and it causes the nuts and bolts of my mind to turn.

What have they planned for me? What am I missing?

I look towards the crackling volts of electricity on the cell bars daring me to escape. And a thought sickens my heart as my hands claw over the knife and tug it beneath my body to conceal it from the cameras.

There *is* a monster out there, the one that gave me this knife, this weapon.

And that means this monster wants me dead.

2

THE REST OF THE night passes in a haze that I scarcely remember, other than one emotion that overrides any of the others coursing through my mind and body.

Fear.

That's the main weapon of the Enclave, after all. It's fear. It's causing fear in the hearts of their enemies, such that they're immobilised from head to toe, unwilling to act.

No one will stage a rebellion now. No one has the guts to do it. And the Enclave is the one that instilled that lack of drive within humanity. That lack of drive for their own freedom, to fight for what they believe in.

I'm fearful because of the weapon that's been chucked into my cell. I get a better look at it when morning arrives and the lights are snapped back on again. The cold seeps into the ventilation system, allowing a warmth to flood the aging cell with all its greyness.

Because of the camera, I keep my body as deathly still as possible, not willing to give anything away. I shield the knife with my body, then glance down at it whilst keeping my head as neutral as possible.

My back aches from the strange posture, but I still every fibre in my body as my eyesight roves.

The knife gleams in the dim light, its shine reflecting right into my eyes. Strangely, it's the brightest thing I've seen in years, considering I never get to see the sun and only those charge-lights slammed into sockets attached to the prison walls.

I pick at knife's handle, as if afraid the thing is going to electrocute me. As if to send a message, the electric cell bars crackle and steam with a vengeance, the blue strands of voltage menacing in their hisses.

Who on earth sent this to me? What is their purpose? Why do they want me framed for something I didn't do? Why are they sending *me* this of all people?

What's the deal here?

As the smell of a conspiracy rushes into my nostrils, I pull the knife out a little, then inspect the metal. The shiny reflection causes me to recall the weapons from my childhood. My father had an entire stash of them in the basement, which held a secret entrance through a dusty old bookshelf so the Enclave inspections didn't find them.

I remember wandering down there one day, when I was a wee little boy, and seeing all the gleaming metals, seeing all the guns and rifles stashed there. The few plasma rifles we had, the electric bolt pistols, too.

But they were nothing against the Enclave, who somehow managed to generate infinite volts through their many power plants dotted throughout the country.

My father had even sent a scout to go look for the Enclave's secret, of how they seemed to create energy without needing any in the first place. But the scout never returned, presumed dead, and that was the end of the matter.

Months later, the Enclave raided our house, snatched my father without another word, and then razed the entire building to the ground. Those weapons were gone, and with it, the chance of a rebellion. The chance of grabbing back our freedoms as human beings.

The Enclave, from that day, were done with portraying a nice image. They were evil, and wanted to make it known to the entirety of Old Britain.

Now, this knife in my hand reminds me of those weapons, reminds me of the dream my father had, a dream I shared and still share. But it's just that, a dream, a far off vision of a utopic nation that has no basis in reality.

And the reality is that someone is trying to frame me for smuggling a weapon in here. And that kind of thing warrants a death sentence. Without questioning.

Footsteps clang down the hall, echoing across the metal surfaces surrounding the prison like ping pong balls from my childhood. I gasp with a panic, then snatch the knife and turn over on my mattress. My left shoulder blocks the camera from viewing the blade, blocks me from an almost certain death.

On the right side of the mattress, there's a little section I discovered a few weeks ago, a tiny hole in the seams. I peel it back, then tuck that knife into the gap, hoping the guard's don't do inspections today.

If it's found, I'm dead. But there isn't much I can do about that.

The guard then arrives. He wears the typical mask that Enclave guards wear, a red demon with black swirls that covered everything but the eyes and the mouth, and holds a baton by his side. The baton is a void-like black, around a metre long, and with a deadly charge that shocks upon contact like an electric punch. The guard's eyes are beady, bloodshot, with hatred spanning every centimetre of those orbs.

He's tall, too. They all are, as if their height has been artificially tampered with to make them more domineering. More able to cause damage. And all the guards speak with such robotic tones that I can't tell if they're trained humans or trained androids programmed to be guards.

"Prisoner 7856b," the guard says in that grating tone I've come to grow used to. "Get up and use the defecation centre. You have two minutes."

That's the way the guards roll around here. They dictate when you rise from the mattress, when you go to the toilet, when you have meals, which way you walk, the pace at which you walk, where you go for the day, what you do in the day. They dictate everything, and there isn't a morning meal, so I battle the rumbles of my stomach as I stalk towards the little basin in the corner.

I can feel the camera to my rear watching me as I pee, then I pull up the orange, near-shredded rags the prison calls clothes and head to the electric bars again.

"You are assigned to Colonel Zambol today," the guard says through the bars. "I will take you to him. Come."

That colonel is in charge of scientific research, which means today I'll likely be helping him mess with patients, or test subjects as he likes to call them. Even those of the Enclave ranks know how much of a madman the scientist is, and that gleam in his eyes whenever he's describing an experiment never fails to send shocks into my brain as to how a man could be so evil.

But he's a part of the Enclave, so I shouldn't be surprised.

Or maybe *I'll* be one of his test subjects, injected with some kind of drug against my will like other prisoners I've seen. It's happened before, and the hallucinations that night were stark and real and frightening to another degree.

In any case, I don't have a choice but to lean into the fear and get on with things. Otherwise, it's death on the spot. And, though I'm the son of Alex Sharp, leader of the old Uprising, I'm not treated specially here.

They're not afraid to kill me, and they've made that known very clearly.

"Step out of the cell," the guard says, once he uses a key to power off the electric bars. He gets his baton out, flicks the switch at its base, then points it at me. The electricity within fizzles in warning. "You remember—any unallowed movements will cause a shock. Two unallowed movements will be two shocks. Three unallowed movements will be enough shocks for death."

I avoid staring at the guard's devil-like mask as I limp through the electric bars that are clear now and allow the guard to position himself behind me. The crackle of the baton is a constant reminder of what could happen as the white, blaringly bright lights of the hallway shock me again.

My cell is in a large wing of other cells arranged in a zig-zag fashion so prisoners can't communicate, with electric prison bars in almost every direction my eyes glance, and every prisoner averts their gaze from meeting anyone else's as they're dragged out of their cells.

Looking at each other, other than at the sanctioned and controlled social times, is a punishable offence, since the Enclave know that an old kind of morse code can be used as communication through blinking.

My father spoke about it once, even demonstrated it with an old friend of his, but the code is long since forgotten. The

Enclave just want another excuse to kill whoever they want and exert their power.

"This way," the guard, who I now name Grate due to his voice, says. With a hand to the back—my back then chills with a shiver—he pushes me towards another hallway with scratch marks from desperate prisoners across the walls.

All throughout the prison, in every hallway that the eye can see, grey is the dominant colour. And not different shades of grey—that would be too much of a personality. Just one, never-ending, dull grey that jabs into my eyes every time I see it. That grey haunts my nightmares every sleep, a reminder of the trap I'm locked in.

I keep a watch out as I'm led through countless corridors. Typically, all the guards lead the prisoners one way, but this time I see a similar-to-Grate-looking guard head inside the cell of a prisoner. Guards never do that, apart from during one thing.

They're conducting searches today.

Searches that, if done properly as the guards always do, can yield that knife someone threw into my cell.

And that means the likelihood that I survive till the night is slimmer than my body from years of starvation and malnutrition.

"This way," the guard says, pointing me to another hallway.

I stumble over, keeping myself as upright as possible since slouching too much is an unallowed movement.

I glance at more cells being entered by guards, and that ultimate emotion breaks out within me. The emotion that the Enclave feeds on like a starving man on a bear he skins with his own hands.

Fear.

3

Colonel Zambol is an angry man. Always angry. His face, if that blob of flesh with more wrinkles than a scratched mattress could even be called a face, is set in a permanent frown, with mouth always ready to bark some order and eyes darker than the night sky I haven't seen in eight years.

He wears a suit, always, made of some mix of carbon fibre and typical clothing fabric. He struts on those knobbly legs around a laboratory filled with acrid smells staining blood-infested metal surfaces that only he finds soothing. And the worst part is the bloody work the man makes us do.

It's back-breaking, pain-inducing, gruelling labour. And yet, for the life of me, I can't work out what the man is planning. What the colonel is making.

Some sort of new weapon that needs the boxes of plasma he has me lugging all day long? Or some new formula of electricity that can tighten the Enclave's hold on the citizens of New Enclave even further?

With men like Zambol, I wonder what motivates them in life. I wonder what they see in the world, whether their eyes are tinted with some kind of evil lens that makes pain pleasurable to them. *Causing* pain, that is.

When he isn't looking, I stare into the back of his skull, into that almost bald head of black hair, wishing I could get revenge for all the souls this man has taken against their will. For all the evil he has done in the world.

But I am powerless in this prison, and he knows it, so doesn't even turn to watch his back whilst the prisoners work.

The painful smell of fumes fills my nostrils once more as I grab another box from the conveyor belt with calloused fingers. Sweat pours from my forehead, so much that it could fill the basin in my cell ten times over. I wipe some of it off with my fingers, balancing the box against my ribs, then hold the box once more.

That only makes my grip on the box more slippery. Too slippery.

It drops.

The noise is deafening, something inside the box smashing like glass, and all the other prisoners stop for the merest second. Their eyes flick to me, and heat tinges my cheeks. I stumble over myself in grabbing the box again, praying Zambol didn't notice.

But I'm too late.

Zambol kicks at my hands, then smacks me in the face with an open palm. I reel back, pain shooting through my body like a wildfire. I glance up at the colonel with hateful eyes, and he is surrounded by two guards, both holding batons, with bolt pistols strapped to their chests in case I try anything.

Fear makes it such that trying something is the last thing on my mind.

"What was that?" Zambol says, voice barely above a whisper. When I don't reply, he stamps a foot on the ground. The metal thumps like a corpse being chucked on a pile of ten others. I flinch, then shiver. "What was that?" he repeats. "Are you not grateful for the work we have given?" His voice rises to a shout by the end, and he turns to whisper to one of the guards. I can't hear a word he says.

The other guard leaves with Zambol, who barks orders at some prisoners to my left. But his voice dilates as the second guard blocks the blaring white lights above. Blocks it with his baton.

The baton strikes my right shoulder, and pain fizzes through my body as the shock races along every single nerve. I cry out, then my arm spasms like some demon has taken hold. My knees hit the floor, then quake as every synapse feels like it's working overtime to transfer the pain from shoulder to shoulder. Then down to my arms. Then my hands, right down to the fingertips.

I feel weak, my hair standing on end from the shock, and sweat stains the ground beneath me. My own sweat. Now falling off my face. As I clutch the metal in desperate fingers.

"Do not commit any more offences," the guard says in such a cool voice the anger within me spikes. But that fear, the same fear the Enclave feasts on, halts any movements resulting from the anger. "Do remember—unallowed movements can result in death if taken far enough."

I clamber to my feet once more, feet that shake with every molecule that moves in my body. My skeleton feels fried, like the sun's been put three metres away and is blasting me with heat.

I spasm as I grab the box once more, the handles almost slipping from my grasp again. But I hold on, just barely, and deposit it on the other conveyor belt which runs into another room where more prisoners are tasked with lugging the boxes.

The box I crashed has disappeared, as if teleported out of the room. More likely is that another prisoner suffered the extra work of hauling it away.

In this place, if one prisoner fails, the rest suffer. One way or another.

One prisoner, for the briefest second, gives me a sympathetic look. I don't catch his features fully, since that would be an offence punishable with another debilitating shock. My eyes drop to the man's hands, and he holds his own box, which he promptly deposits before hurrying away.

All I remember is that singular scar on the back of his hand, a jagged line of flesh. A scar that disappears beneath the sleeve of his prison clothes, and I assume it goes all the way to his shoulder.

I have similar scars across my body. Rites of honour is the way I view them. Littering almost every inch of my body, like someone's playing noughts and crosses—an old game my father and I used to enjoy before the Uprising failed—with my body.

I stumble over the laboratory floor to reach the boxes again. From what I understand, these boxes are filled with some chemical compound that Zambol needs when rolling out large scale experiments. Experiments that can help the Enclave tighten its noose over the citizens of New Enclave.

The boxes could house plasma, some electricity stores, or something else to create weapons that will terrorise the citizens further. The Enclave is in an arm's race with itself as to how far it can push pain-causing technology.

The reason Zambol runs his operation from the prison is because we're easy test subjects. Easy to reach, and easy to control since we're already trapped as it is. That makes us easy to observe too, since under the threat of a baton smack, we'll do anything.

I'm hauling what seems the thousandth box when Zambol gives another shout. A piercing shout.

"Someone is here for Prisoner 7856b," he screams across the room. None of the other prisoners drop their boxes, but I'm not like the other prisoners. I'm the one that capitulates at the worst moments, and this is another one of them.

I drop the box. The metal pings. Then I clamp a hand over my mouth and glance up. Zambol is staring right at me, as if he knows my prisoner number and face by heart. His eye twitches as he looks down at the box, but a cool expression flows over his face. As if emotions are electric switches he can turn on and off.

"Someone pick that up," Zambol barks. "Prisoner 7856b, go over there." His thin finger points to the exit, where two guards are waiting. But waiting for what? "*Now*, if you will, or there will be consequences."

I break out of the trance that overtook me and hurry across the laboratory, bare feet almost slipping against the chilled metal. I reach the door and those two guards are staring at me from the hallway.

Their eyes are beady as always, expression hidden beneath red masks, and their hands hold batons at the ready.

Am I in for another beating? But Zambol would've just done it in front of the other prisoners if it was a beating.

"You are being requested by Colonel Raze," one guard says, tone as robotic as ever.

My back immediately freezes up, my mind jumping to the worst conclusions. Because no one ever gets called by Raze, unless—unless they've committed the most heinous of offences.

Raze is the main handler of the prison, the man at the top. The man where all the evil in this place originates from.

And he never speaks to anyone, much less requests for them. Unless they've done something gravely wrong. Unless they're being called for a special execution.

As a guard grabs my arm, causing me to wince from the spark of pain, and hauls me through the corridor, I remember the weapon thrown into my cell last night.

Crap. The guards are doing cell inspections today. How could I be so stupid? I should've gotten rid of it when I had the chance, for God's sake.

They must've found the weapon, and now they're calling me over to discuss the punishment. Discuss what the best way to kill me would be. The way most warning to the other prisoners, to deter them from attempting the same offence.

I let my feet drag across the floor. My last moments are up, like my mother's old timer that sat on her bedside desk trickling the last dregs of brown sand.

Mason Sharp, killed by the same people who'd murdered his entire family.

I'm about to meet my end. In the worst way possible.

4

COLONEL RAZE'S OFFICE IS the closest room to the roof of the prison, at least that's what my intuition tells me. The fear of meeting the man causes my sense of direction to fall in on itself like a collapsing star. I'm more confused than anything, but the guards dump me outside a cold looking metal door, in an empty hallway, before turning back and leaving.

They disappear behind a corner, into a hallway leading to the main staircase we ascended, the harsh lighting above me glaring down as if foreboding my fate. I shiver, though I'm not cold. The chill is in my heart, instead.

The guards leave me here because they know—the fear from the Enclave is so debilitating that I won't move, I won't budge from my place. I'll do exactly as they say.

And I do. As the smell of antiseptic walls mixed with the fumes of my own destruction fill my nose, I stare at those metallic double doors that hide Colonel Raze's office. The grey swirls before me, as if some kind of time machine, and I wish I had one.

I wish I could go back and tell my father of that ploy of the Enclave, tell him to get out with the rest of my family, and continue the Uprising. But one mistake can end a whole movement, and it had.

A bolt clicking back alerts my attention. The double doors open with ominous scratches across the metal flooring, gusts of mist rising from the ground, and electric charges buzz at me from the other side.

Raze is there, visible through the electricity, his wrinkled face much like Zambol's. His eyes are hooded, always hiding his emotions as he peers between the gaps in the electric gate. He flicks a switch on the other side, and the electricity dies.

I let out a breath I didn't know I'd been holding. But immediately I suck in another gulp of air. Raze steps through the doors and faces me, and I see the wisps of hair on his almost shaven chin. His eyes are searching, interrogating, and search mine.

For what, I don't know. And that's what scares me the most. Not knowing his intentions, not knowing what I'd been called in for. Not knowing if I'd be alive by the end of this meeting.

"Let us head inside, shall we?" Raze says, gesturing towards the disabled electric gate.

I glance to the sides of the double doors, almost out of instinct. I don't think I could handle another shock. It would likely immobilise me for the rest of the day, such is the pain.

"There is no switch on this side," Raze says. "Be assured. Now, through the doors please, or I shall have to call some of the guards to come. And we both do not want that to occur, do we?"

He has this grandfather persona that sickens me more than a bolt shot to the stomach. I comply, shuffling through the doors. I'm not electrocuted, thankfully, and enter his office, enter a level of warmth that sizzles my nerves.

Raze switches the gate back on, and the electricity crackles behind me once more. Raze stalks around the circular room to his seat at a desk in the office's centre, roving over the shelves surrounding the sides whilst doing so.

It's the first time I've been in here, and the place looks…rather typical for an office, at least from what I remember. Apart from the body parts lying in showcases to my left, with tags attached to them. And the weapons lying across the room as if haphazardly chucked there. And the disgusting husk of humanity that works from the office.

Attached to the pieces of flesh are prisoner tags, I realise with a startle, and that familiar shiver courses over my spine. I attempt to breathe calmly, despite knowing my end is nigh.

Mason Sharp, gone with not even a whimper, but a silence. A pitiful silence.

"Take a seat, Mason," Raze says, and I struggle to hide the shock as I stare at the leather chair he's pointing to. It looks too soft, and I fear I'd sink into the fabric and never get out. "Today would be appropriate, Mason."

He used my name twice, the grandfather persona kicking in, and my guard is up again.

I almost fall over as I dump myself into the seat, and struggle not to groan from the contact. This is a luxury I haven't felt in over eight years. The simplicity of fabric cradling one's body is a foreign feeling for us prisoners.

But then I remember why I'm actually here. To meet my end. To be dragged over to the other side of death at the hands of my enemies.

"You are here for an important reason," Raze says.

I clamp my lips together. Unwilling to speak. Unwilling to let anything loose, such is the fear.

"An important reason because we have questions to ask, and by we I mean the Enclave of course." Raze sends me a piercing gaze, his stormy grey eyes flashing with the threat of what he could do to me should I not answer truthfully.

My eyes leave his and drop to the two batons leaning against the wall. Above those, hooked onto spikes dug into the wall, is a large knife. Gleaming in the white light glistening from the ceiling, tip sharper than an electric buzz.

God, what the heck's gonna happen to me?

"Our questions regard something of interest to us," Raze continues, not noticing, or merely unwilling to comment on, my staring at the weapons. "It is of interest to us because of reasons I shall not tell you. Not that you deserve to be told of course. But you may have information, and I want your full cooperation, do you understand?"

I look back at him now, and see the need for a verbal answer.

"I understand."

"And just to make sure we are operating the same—not giving a satisfactory answer shall result in worse than death. Is that, too, understood?"

I nod. Then, when he doesn't continue, say, "I understand."

Raze laughs, a throaty rumbling that sets me at even more of an unease. He grabs a cigar from next to his little tablet and shoves that into his mouth. Blows some smoke onto my face, and I do all I can not to gag from the turbulent smell.

"Do you know what tempus is?" Raze asks. "And I want you to answer me truthfully, Mason. I need the truth. The Enclave requires the truth, understand?"

"I understand."

"Tempus—do you have any knowledge of what it is? Where it can be found?"

I've always been able to read faces, at least to some extent. Of course people like Raze are trained in hiding their true intentions, their true emotions. But I can tell he's worried, I can tell the Enclave's worried.

Or if less than worry, a mere apprehension. And the thought makes me feel a remnant of happiness, despite the very real chance that I meet my end today.

"I've never heard of it," I say, telling the truth. "Never heard of it in my life."

Raze leans forward. Blasts me with another wave of sickening smoke. "Do you wish to know one of Zambol's experimental interests?"

I blink at the response, not saying a word. I don't have to as Raze continues.

"He wishes to understand pain. Immense pain. He wishes to categorise such pain. It will help the Enclave in unimaginable ways. We shall...be able to level the pain to such an exact degree as to gain whatever we wish." Raze jerks his large head over to the showcase on our left. I don't look, since I saw it before—pieces of flesh, with prisoner tags attached to them. "It is strange, for all the advancements we have made, we cannot create life anew. Limbs lost will, alas, always be lost. Remember that, Mason, when you answer. I am certain Zambol will appreciate new limb donors to carry out his pain experiments on."

Raze leans back, and I lean back too. I read somewhere, when I was a child, that adopting a relaxed position could induce a relaxed state, sort of like tricking my brain to do what I want.

That author was a total liar, the book a hoax. Somewhere in my mind I hear the screams of those prisoners who'd lost body parts to scientists like Zambol, and that familiar shiver fires up again. That familiar fear that races through all prisoners.

"Ready to answer the way we wish?" Raze asks.

I nod. "Yes."

"Good. Now, I want you to listen to me carefully, and choose your answer carefully." This time, Raze grabs a bolt pistol from a holster on his belt and places it on the table. It clanks, the metal tempered to be harder than diamonds. Streamlined to perfection to allow volts to shoot through its barrel with an efficiency unimaginable. "Answer carefully," Raze says, one hand on the barrel with the other holding his cigar.

"I do not know anything about tempus," I say, staring at him, right in the eyes. He searches my gaze for what feels the hundredth time, then leans back again.

Then all at once, he grabs the pistol and dives over the table with his torso. His hands scrunch the collar of my ragged shirt, yank to pull me closer. My neck strangles, eyes wide. I strain against the pull, but Raze's grip is iron-clad.

"I want the truth, Mason," Raze says. He licks his lips, the cigar forgotten on his table. The pistol pushes into my skull, digging like an undertaker preparing a grave. "One shot and you're dead, you understand?"

"Won't you just kill me anyway?" I say, for once disregarding the debilitating fear. I realise it was a mistake to say that.

Raze smacks my temple with the gun. Though the pistol is light, the metal is anything but dull. My mind pings from the contact, consciousness swirling before me. Another hit to the cheek brings me back into reality with a gasp, and my eyes focus in on the intense hatred in Raze's gaze.

"Answer me properly," Raze says. "Answer me truthfully. You father knew about tempus, and you are telling me that you do not? His father's puppet, that's what you are." Raze's eyes look like they're about to expand and explode. Raze's voice is controlled in a devilish way, a terrifying way. "I know you know what tempus is. I know you know what it does. Tell me the truth, Mason. Tell me what you know, *now*."

I didn't even know that my father knew about tempus. I don't know what it is, never even heard of it. But Raze clearly isn't going to take that as an answer.

The cold touch of the gun still perforates my skull, and my voice comes out gurgled from the strangling.

"I don't know," I say. "My…my father never said—said anything about tempus. I don't—I don't know, for God's sake."

Raze laughs, then leans back and lets out another laugh, more demonic than the first. He reaches over for an e-phone, a hologram that pops up whilst attached to his tablet, and makes a request.

The request chills me to the core.

"Bring the guards in. And bring them in now. Two or three should be enough." Raze gives me a sinful smile, threat laced within. "I want to turn my office into one of Zambol's little games."

5

THE WORLD SWIRLS AROUND me, swirls like consciousness is a bird from my youth, those beautiful animals with wings that let them fly. I always wished to be like them as they soared above us. I remember, as that sliver of consciousness eludes me, our little townhouse, with the grass fluttering and the scent of honey lacing the still air. Life seemed perfect, suspended in time, with the only moving thing that little bird flying above Old Britain.

The air was cool, and I breathed it in like it contained my life force, fresh with every gulp. I could never catch the bird, never grasp it no matter how hard I reached into the sky. We humans were rooted to the ground, unable to escape the dangers that chased us. Only able to face them head on.

And then that image fades, and I smell that sickening antiseptic once more. My arms are on the ground, cold and quivering, and crimson stains the metal flooring. A dark red that causes my eyes to widen, and I realise the blood I'm lying in is my own.

My eyes roll into my mind as I search through what happened before I blacked out. Raze...he'd questioned me, hadn't he? Questioned me about something called tempus, something I had no idea about. I'd...told him the truth, that I didn't know, and then he'd beaten me.

Then those guards. Those guards had done something. They'd—that's right, they'd pressed their batons against my arm, right from the wrist up to the shoulder, slowly pulling it up as more shocks raked my body.

But these shocks were different, more tempered, more measured, as if carefully crafted to a volume of pain. Each shock growing worse and worse as those same questions flooded out from Raze like a torrent of rainwater—do I know what tempus is, do I know what it does, where it can be found, what my father knew of tempus?

And...I must've answered truthfully, since now I'm here, back in Zambol's lair, facing the floor, smelling the smell of my own rotten flesh mixed with the basin back in my cell.

My eyes clear, and I hear prisoners shuffling across the ground, completely ignoring me. That's what we've been trained to do, desensitized to the sight of another prisoner lying on the floor, seemingly dead, in a pool of their own blood.

My heart pounds a million times a second, and a headache roars through me. But I get the signal, the reason why I've been put back in here.

I'm expected to continue working, and I get up and get back to hauling boxes despite the damage to my arms and pain wracking every inch of my body. I shove the boxes onto the opposite conveyor belt under the gleeful watch of Zambol and his crowd of guards. Each guard stares at us, stares at the boxes we deposit and look for any damages for which to punish us.

And Zambol's thin, sickly smile causes another wave of rage to almost push me over the edge. I remember what Raze said about Zambol's experiments—on documenting pain, and I glance at those boxes I'm hauling over.

Do they contain something for those experiments? Some secret chemical we don't know a thing about?

I wish to crack open a box and take a look inside with a charged flashlight I don't have, but I'm a prisoner. Trapped. With no name and only a number to identify me attached to the bottom of my shirt as a fraying tag.

The humanity has been stripped from me, and it's something I must understand to survive here for the rest of my life, before death arrives as it does for all. Even the Enclave haven't found a stop for that.

As I'm hauling back another box, my gaze slips down to my right arm, and I see the wound setting in. It's reddish, almost hellish, with spots of pink screaming out for help. It's not properly dug into the pale skin yet, but the signs of a scar are there.

A scar that runs from wrist all the way to shoulder, about the width of a baton—

There's someone else with that scar. That prisoner I'd seen before, the one who gave me a sympathetic look before after that guard had shocked me with his baton. That prisoner—God, I should've seen his tag—must've been questioned as well, interrogated as to what tempus is.

I need to find him, need to talk to him. Need to unravel this mystery surrounding tempus.

If the Enclave are worried about it, the signal is clear. It's something of deadly importance, something my father was looking into, and something I have to uncover if I'm to keep that dimmer-than-a-void dream alive.

I haul another box over, all the while my eyes rove the other prisoners, the air turning a heady, charged scent. I face away from the guards so they can't see me, and make sure the cameras are swivelled towards the other conveyor belt.

At first I don't find him, searching through the sea of orange rags and skeleton-like bodies at the whistling conveyor belt to find a hint of a scar similar to mine. All the prisoners mesh into one crowd of orange, and my eyes continue digging.

And then I do find the man.

And he's looking right at me.

As soon as our gazes meet, his eyes drop to my arm, to the wound, and he gives a nod. Almost imperceptible, but the nod is there. Clear as an old flare.

He was asked the same, interrogated just as I was. Punished just as I was.

I step towards him, head still down, looking out of the periphery of my vision.

But he merely shakes his head, again the signal almost unnoticeable. Then he rushes off to grab another box, and I grab my own box from the same conveyor belt's other end.

We're separated, but the connection is there. That prisoner and I have a link—both being interrogated by the Enclave about something that scares them, something that they *fear*.

That fear is a weakness to exploit. If only I could find out what in the Old Britain tempus is.

My mind is whirring like electricity being charged, theories flying as to who that man is with the intense eyes, with the scar on his arm the same as mine. His scar has set in pretty deep, meaning tempus has been clawing at the Enclave for a long time.

And I'm the freshest prisoner to get a dose of their interrogation.

I return to dragging boxes over, ignoring the pain soaring through my body—the shocks to my arm from the earlier beating, and the stabs of hurt coursing through every other part of my frame.

My mind flits over to that weapon in my cell, the knife chucked in by someone anonymous, in the middle of the night. The weapon that had filled my heart with a dread that nothing else could. The dread of imminent death.

The fact that I've not been called out by the guards yet, given that most of the day has elapsed, means they didn't catch the knife hidden in the seams of my mattress. If they had been the ones to frame me, they would've found it easily by now.

And I'd be a dead man.

So, no guards under orders from the Enclave to frame the son of the old Uprising's leader. That leaves a possibility that both frightens me as much as it fuels me.

What if it's another prisoner? What if it's someone who has the ability to melt with the shadows of Enclave Prison and visit other cells? Blend in with the prison, and return without getting caught?

Someone with a power the Enclave fear.

And that's a power we could all use whilst inside this prison.

What seems like hours later but could just be minutes—the sense of time within the prison halls are more warped than a hologram—we're all called over for a meal. Well, dragged over would be a more accurate way of putting it.

Guards, since we eat meals within the walls of our cells, haul me away to mine, as they do every day, my feet scrap- ing against the chilly metal floors. I hear another prisoner get electrocuted by a baton, probably for not allowing himself to be dragged like an animal to a slaughtering. His shouts ping off the wall to reach the rest of the prisoners, the rest of us. As a threat of the consequences of non-compliance.

I shuffle along with the guards, then sneak a glance to my left. There, in cell 6541a, is that prisoner from before. The one with the scar, the one who was questioned just like I was. The number and letter is also on his orange prison clothes, on a tag attached to the bottom. I give him the barest of a glance, then look away. Looking too closely will warrant another punishment.

I need to speak with him. But I don't know how. In these hallowed prison halls, with the thickets of guards surrounding every nook and cranny of the prison walkways, talking is a privilege we don't have.

But I have to find a way. Because if there's something the Enclave fear, it's something powerful we can use.

Use to break out of this place and start the second Uprising, and take down the Enclave for good.

But of course, far-fetched dreams will always remain that—far-fetched. And that sense of defeat rubs into me once more as the guards chuck me into the cell with a bowl of schlop and activate the electric gate again.

It buzzes. I sit down, on the cold metal flooring, and tuck into the food. It's disgusting, but I need the energy. But for what—

Well, that's what I'm about to find out.

6

INSPECTIONS HAPPEN AROUND EVERY week or so, though I don't know when that week starts and ends. I've averaged it out to every five days over the last hundred or so days. Since the guards didn't catch the knife, I've got about four days to find somewhere to hide it before the guards crack down.

In case it wasn't obvious, a weapon in a cell entails certain death for the prisoner. I won't even die as Mason Sharp, son of Alex Sharp. I'll die as a random prisoner, annexed to the history books as some figure in a spreadsheet on a prison computer somewhere.

I slept less the last night. Whoever chucked me the knife might have been roaming the prison halls. I'm sure it wasn't a guard, which means another prisoner. A powerful prisoner, if they can slip into the prison shadows and travel its halls under the cover of darkness. And not get caught in the process.

I wish I had that ability—then I could break out of here and get justice for my people. Or, that so-called justice that my father always spoke of during another one of his dinner-time spiels. Of how we have to usurp the Enclave and their oppression.

But then replace it with what? Our own form of oppression? What if the people we help end up against us, and then another Uprising occurs? And it becomes a cycle, over and over again. Death and destruction for eternity.

But what other option do we have?

My mind flits back to the prisoner with the scar on his arm. A similar scar is slowly forming for me, the flesh hardening with every pulse of pain Raze and his guards caused. That prisoner, 6541a with the piercing eyes, was asked about tempus. That means he's someone important, someone that an alliance with will benefit.

If only I could get a chance to speak with him.

The next day passes as normal. I'm woken by the coolness sucked through the vents and making way for a stifling heat, a guard shouting through the electric gate to rouse me, in addition to the fizz of said gate.

I pretend to wake, since I was already conscious, then finger the space to my right, along that little ripped seam next to the mattress. I shift my body over to hide what I'm doing from the camera and the guard.

The knife is still there. I'm safe for another day.

I defecate when the guard tells me to, well within the two minute time limit, then follow the guard outside. We're hauling more boxes today, which ignites that curiosity within me once more as to what Zambol is trying to accomplish. Raze mentioned pain experiments—but why would that be necessary for the Enclave?

To torture more?

And where does tempus fall into all that?

I don't know, and a part of me doesn't wish to find out, in all honesty. Because knowledge can be dangerous. And clearly, it can paint a target on your back, a target for those who seek that knowledge.

But there is one good thing about hauling boxes for Zambol. That prisoner from before might be called again to work there, Prisoner 6541a, meaning I might get the chance to speak with him. Ask him what the hell tempus is.

But he isn't there. For the entirety of the morning—what I assume to be morning anyway since we don't have watches or clocks with us—he isn't present.

A sickening feeling, as I stand on blood stains on the rough flooring of the lab and sniff toxic chemicals, settles in my heart.

Have they got him? Have they pincered him because he knows something about tempus?

I don't want to think about the possibility, because tempus, whatever it actually is, is important. It's the first ray of light in these dark halls in years and years, and not something I can give up so easily.

I continue to haul boxes, the smell of prisoner sweat stifling in addition to the heat sticking to the rags I wear. The shirt sticks to my scrawny chest, wrapping over each rib like funeral clothes. As if all this work is really just digging my own grave.

My muscles are burning, scar pounding as if being shocked again, and I'm breathing in gasps, and my eyes are almost bleeding from the effort of staying upright with no food in the morning.

And Zambol just stands there at the end, smug smile tugging at his wrinkles. He gives me a jerk of the head, eyes flashing, and I hurry to the conveyor belt to deposit the box despite the exhaustion.

I don't drop the box this time. I got the warning yesterday, of a baton shock. And it's a lesson learned. I return for more boxes, that wound on my arm still pulsing strong. My legs hurt since they have the brunt of the work, carrying me to and fro across the room.

And all throughout, I glance towards that metal door leading out of the lab, wondering where on earth that prisoner is. Has he been killed, sacked off the moment the Enclave found out he has an inkling of what tempus is?

Or maybe, if he's the one that roams the nights of the prison, he merely escaped, saving himself rather than the rest of us.

But I'm wrong on both ideas.

Because then he arrives, through that metal door which opens with a deathly grate. I watch for a second, then my head snaps down, and my legs hurry across to the conveyor belt with the box in hand. But I don't forget what I see.

How can I?

That prisoner's face, Prisoner 6451a, is beaten in as bad as my arm is. I glance down once more, at the grazed flesh across my forearm, and wince, then grab another box. I need to keep busy so I don't think about it, but his face flashes in my mind once more.

Those piercing eyes, eyes that speak of knowing more than the prisoner lets on, are gaunt now. Destroyed from within, from something that I don't know about. The prisoner limps over, and I watch his bare feet as I cross the room.

Wounds line the centre of his feet, too. Like scraggly sticks wedged beneath his skin. Or like electric shocks from the baton laid down the arches of his foot, as if he was forced to step on an electric wire.

The prisoner doesn't acknowledge me, doesn't acknowledge anyone, and merely continues working as if nothing is the problem. Every few seconds, at least whenever I glance at him, he flinches, twitches as the aftershocks still grip him.

The mere memory of a punishment can induce the punishment itself. And that is a scarier thought than anything.

I haul another box over, arms begging for rest, then turn. And as I do, my eyes rise, and meet the gaze of that prisoner once more. A tension flares in the air, a stifling heat that wraps over me. I know I shouldn't be looking at him, communicating with my eyes.

So, the moment is brief.

And the message coming from him is clear.

To stay away from tempus, stay away from finding the truth. To stop my search for a way to escape and get justice once more for Old Britain.

Because if I continue to find the truth, and succeed in my mission, I could suffer the same fate as him. Beaten to a pulp, and then sent back to work like a dog in a slave house of a prison.

And that, perhaps, is worse than death itself.

I shift over the room again, waiting for the next batch of boxes to arrive through the conveyor belt. My hands are by my side, too tired to raise themselves until the next box comes through. I glance left, notice no one there, and the metal sheen on the wall glares at me. Then a right glance reveals Prisoner 6541a.

His left shoulder is leaned towards me, slightly declined compared to his other shoulder, and I know he can't speak due to the cameras here. If any of them catch him or me communicating, we're both dead.

And the Enclave do not give second chances, nor do they give benefits of the doubt.

In fact, I have a feeling the only reason we're being kept alive is because they reckon we know something about this tempus.

Once they know I don't, they'll kill me off without hesitation if I step out of line.

The next batch of boxes arrive, and I grab mine. Then, Prisoner 6541a grabs his, and my gaze slides down to his fingers that clutch the handles of the box.

He's holding his left index finger up. Just that one finger, instead of wrapping it around the box handles like the rest of the fingers on his hand.

It's a message, subtle, silent yet loud and clear. He takes the box, then turns to me fully. The finger is still left open, and I quickly grab my box. I need to make it seem like I haven't seen anything. Need to make it so that Zambol hasn't a reason to suspect me.

Prisoner 6541a drags himself and his box over to the other conveyor belt, and I do the same a few paces down to make it seem we aren't connected. I stumble, but the box doesn't drop. A tiredness rakes my legs like thousands of electric shocks to the hamstrings.

A sickly smell, of my own blood and sweat mixing in the stifling heat, floods my nostrils like a tsunami. My vision blurs as an immense pain wracks my head. I deposit the box, stand still for a moment, regaining my bearings as the world swirls around me.

A guard shouts at me to continue, threatening a baton strike if I stop. I grab another box, ignoring the sensation that my insides are floating—likely from the immense workload and hunger. I can taste the schlop across my tongue, and yearn it despite the nastiness it's coated with.

But all throughout the rest of the day, well into the afternoon and evening, that bony little finger being stretched out on its own flashes into my vision like some memory of the past, or some weird dream resurfacing midday.

I wonder what Prisoner 6541a meant by that finger.

And I wonder, when I find out, what the consequences are going to be.

7

THE NIGHT IS SHARP, blackness like a solid wall above me, to the right, to the left, and below. As I lie on my mattress, with nothing but a rag of a cover weighing my body down, I feel as if I can't even move up for a second. That black wall of my cell, it seems, has rooted me to this position. I look to my left, see the basin's silhouette where I defecated before I slept under the watchful eye and orders of guards. This has become my life. This prison has consumed me whole.

The air is still, and my thin inhalations reveal the typical smell of antiseptic and metallic eeriness, a smell that is now infused with my nostrils after all these years. The darkness then swirls, as if my mind is searching through it for something to hold onto.

I find some memories way back that pierce the silence. I remember other smells, nicer smells, of daisies and daffodils that we grew in our back garden, in the little greenhouse my father had built with his own hands using wooden slats and window panels when I was a mere baby. Me and my mother often went inside whilst my father was out on Uprising work. We'd peruse all the little flowers my mother had planted, grab a few tomatoes and potatoes from the ones that had grown, and water the rest of the crops without a fuss.

Self-sufficiency—that's what my father preached. Once someone had self-sufficiency and independence, they couldn't be bought with anything so long as they remained principled.

The darkness, then, had almost been non-existent, apart from the spaces between the pockets of stars we could see in the night sky. In its place was a brilliant natural light from the sun that I haven't witnessed in years.

Another memory jumps to the fore, of a school play we did when I was ten years old. I can't remember the story, nor the lines I was memorising, nor anything else actually, not even the people I was acting with. The Enclave heavily censors schools now, but did even back then. It was only in areas where the rebel sentiment was popular that plays and books and art could survive.

Now, I haven't an idea what happened to all those things. Censored into obscurity, my gut tells me.

All I remember from that play was glancing towards the back of the audience whilst sipping a water bottle as I got ready to come on stage. My father and mother were there, staring at me with proud smiles on their faces. Smiles that showed them how much I really meant to them. That, despite the overarching objective of defeating the Enclave and freeing the country, their child's school play held importance in their hearts.

Here, in this prison, my identity has been stripped from me. I am no longer son, person, friend—I am merely Prisoner 7856b. These memories of the glorious past give me an identity, something to clutch onto in these dark moments, and I would fight to hell and back to make sure that the Enclave don't find a way to diminish the last husks of humanity I have left.

Still, there isn't much more than husks remaining amongst the dark abyss that surrounds me. Despite the almost eternal darkness, I struggle to sleep, my senses always on high alert. More than once during the night, I shift my hand towards the ripped seam in my mattress, finger that knife that was thrown in not two days ago.

The next inspection should be within three days, meaning I have to find a way to dispose of this thing before it gets me killed. I finger that knife again now, feel the cold metal race a chilling tinge across my skin. I haven't felt the power to cause death in a long time, and the surge of energy brimming in my fingers is both alarming and strengthening, in ways I can't describe more than that.

Then a rattle catches my attention. A little ping that pops through the silence, and my heart jumps into my throat.

A guard coming for me? What could it be?

I sit up a little, finger still gripping that knife as if, when a guard attacks, I can use it as self-defence. That's even more of a death sentence than anything I can imagine.

My eyes dart towards the black hallway lit dimly by the crackling electric charges on the prison bars. That deadly blue crackle taunts me, daring me to come near so it can ensnare me in its venomous grip. It's as if the Enclave have, somehow, infused some limited kind of consciousness into the electric weapons they have—I know it's impossible, yet my heart wonders, for just a moment.

Another ping rings through the night, low enough that those sleeping likely never heard it. Likely never even knew it occurred.

But I do. I'm part of that special group that hears the noises at night.

The guards don't patrol the nights typically, I've found out over the years. Not because the Enclave don't have the numbers, but more so as a point against the prisoners—that we're so well-imprisoned that guarding us with patrols would be useless.

That ping turns to footsteps, footsteps that rapidly grow louder and louder.

Is this a special guard patrol that the Enclave are running after asking prisoners about tempus, whatever it is? Are they inspecting again to see if any of the prisoners are sleeping or not, incriminating those who aren't?

I shove my head into the mattress—well, my sorry excuse for a mattress—and will myself to sleep. But it doesn't work, and then a bright flash overtakes the blackness of my eyelids, causing a blood red to bleed into the darkness.

My heart doesn't just jump into my throat, it positively bashes my neck with every ounce of strength it has in each beat. I don't dare open my eyes as the flash fades, the coppery scent of my own imminent demise proliferating in my nostrils. I can taste flesh, and blood, then recognise that I've bit into the side of my cheek.

Then, the flash dies, and I realise that my hand is wrapped around the seam in my mattress, where the knife is stored. I was getting ready to battle, unconsciously, my body reacting to danger without the knowledge of my brain.

I...don't know how to interpret the motion, so shove the thought to the back of my head.

When the light fades, my eyes open and search the darkness, groping through for some semblance of grip on reality.

A figure is out there, in the hallway, a silhouette in the dimness. Undetected, somehow, beyond the electric gate. Though, I can make out the orange suit indicating a prisoner, and, in the murky light, the scar across the arm. The scar that runs from the wrist and forearm all the way to the upper shoulder.

It's Prisoner 6541a, the one who'd shown me his finger when in Zambol's laboratory slaving away with all the other prisoners. And now he's here, outside my cell, in the depths of the chilling Enclave night, for a reason I can't fathom.

I shove my head back into the pillow. This must be some sort of trick my mind is playing on me, some twisted level of play that I could have never seen coming. A shock tactic to force me back into the submission that characterises my relationship with the Enclave for the last eight years.

What if they—*the Enclave*—are the ones administering this hallucination?

The thought chills me more than the freeze squeezing through the air ducts to stifle me. The next words spewing from Prisoner 6541a's mouth make things worse.

"Use the knife," he says. "Cut the electric."

It's the first words I've ever heard from him, since he isn't there at the carefully watched and sanctioned social times we have every week. His voice isn't whiny, but a little squeaky, with the undertones of baritone buried deep beneath hours and hours of torture. It's a stretched voice, one that has suffered one too many times yet still risks the danger of roaming the prison at night under the threat of execution.

"Cut it, Mason," Prisoner 6541a says.

My breath hitches, and the temperature clings to me with a greater hold. It's the first time I've heard my name said without malice…well, since I was dragged to this prison all those years ago. It's like an unfamiliar sound, something otherworldly in a way, representing a past utopia that I cannot grasp.

"Mason, get the knife and cut. *Quickly*. We are running out of time."

Lord knows what's gotten into me, but I turn and grip the knife's hilt in steadier fingers than I ought to have. I climb out of bed, risking a glance back at the camera that is now sullen and pointed at the ground like a corpse, then hold the knife to the electric gate.

The metal shimmers, then glistens, then glints into my eye. The electricity dares me to touch it and risk a spasm, or two, or five. If I slice through, wouldn't the electricity zing along the metal and rupture every ounce of skin in my body?

"The knife, Mason," Prisoner 6541a says, wounds on his face from earlier contorting like electric spasms. "It's…*tempus*. Use it and cut through." Under the new levels of light close to the electricity, I spot worry in the man's eyes. Worry and the hint of urgency, though for what I can't understand.

"Use it, Mason, goddammit."

That gets me into gear, and out of my whirring mind. I close my eyes and slice the knife, and find the electric gate subsides as if waves of an ocean being held up to allow a path through the middle—a resemblance of an old story I remember my mother telling me about when I was a child.

"Quickly, now," Prisoner 6541a says, grabbing my wrist where the wound and oncoming scar is, and dragging me out through the now clear doorway. "This should reset in a few seconds, so we need to quickly leave." Prisoner 6541a then flashes that bright beam of light again, for a reason I don't know, then lowers the light to his side.

"Come this way," Prisoner 6541a says, jerking his head towards the massive compound to our left, where a labyrinth of hallways indicates the many prison facilities.

I glance back at my cell, at the defunct electric gate that will apparently reignite in a few seconds. I could run back inside and return to my life of obedience and submission to something that doesn't deserve it—to something that killed my whole family, everyone I knew and loved. To something that destroyed the hopes of my people for a future they could believe in, for a future they could actually *live*, rather than survive.

Or, I could follow this Prisoner 6541a into the unknown, no matter how bright—or dark—it could be.

I watch as the electric gate roars back to life, the crackling attempting to taunt me once more. But this time I'm on the right side, on the safe side, and feel a coolness that's soothing and not biting as I turn to face Prisoner 6541a.

"Take me where you want," I say. "I'm done with this."

8

THE KNIFE PULSES IN my fingers as I follow Prisoner 6541a through the darkened hallways of the prison. Thin lights wrap around the upper edges of each hallway and large room we enter, all the while my eyes glance left and right, peering into the cells of the other prisoners. They don't know that I'm here—they sleep, somewhat oddly given where we are, in a safety that I've shed for this random man I don't know in a place where one wrong move can result in almost certain death.

The air smells of fumes—not because something is on fire, but rather I can smell the flames of my own destruction singeing my body as if in warning. The entire compound is set to an eerie cool. Not as cold as the cells being fizzed by the icy ventilation, yet not as warm as when undergoing back-breaking labour at the hands of the Enclave.

Despite the fact that all manner of hazards lie in wait—security guards and cameras and electric gates being three of the least severe—I feel oddly at peace, at a comfort I never would've thought of.

The knife in my hand, clasped tightly ever since I'd taken it out of the seam of my mattress, surges power through me. Surges a conviction that I haven't felt in so long as my feet lightly hit the metal flooring as we pass the labyrinth of cells.

"Where are we going?" I ask Prisoner 6541a, to which he replies with a stony silence. He lays a finger against his lips as his eyes search mine, as if looking for some semblance of humanity that most of the other prisoners lack.

"Follow," he whispers. "Questions later."

I nod, not understanding why I trust this man. Perhaps it is the shared experience of being tortured by the Enclave for information on something called tempus—which Prisoner 6541a referred as being my knife earlier, whatever that truly means.

We pass another winding hallway, filled with cells on each side, teeming as if rats in a sewer starving for food. Cells aren't shared in this facility. It was at one point, my father told me when I was younger—but cannibalism became a rife problem, and the quantity of human slaves decreased at a rapid rate. Hence the solitary confinement with closely guarded social times where feeding on each other was not a possibility.

Still, despite the typical estrangement, a familiarity passes between me and Prisoner 6541a, and I wish to ask him his real name. But the moment of asking passes as a turn reaches us, marked by a slab of grey brick with a slant of light reaching across it to find us a cobbled path.

I try to turn the corner, but Prisoner 6541a grabs my shoulder and wrenches me back. He presses another finger to his lips, his eyes narrowed, lets go of my shoulder, then points to a corner of the room I was about to enter.

A thin red dot stares back at me, and under it is a camera. Not unlike the one in my room, likely fitted with an infrared lens so it can detect things even in the silent darkness.

Prisoner 6541a pulls out a device from his pocket, then presses a button against its side. I can't get a good look at the device, as a moment later the world lights up with the brightness of a thousand suns bursting at once. A white flash that momentarily blinds me.

I cover my eyes with a forearm, then add the other for good measure. The knife feels hotter in my hand, then the redness of my eyelids slowly fades as the light returns to normal.

"Sorry," Prisoner 6541a says, the first semblance of humanity I've seen from the man, other than being a fellow prisoner. "Light always gets the eyes."

I nod. It got my eyes all right, but it also had the same effect as back in my cell.

For a reason I can't fathom, the camera looks struck by an extreme sorrow, its head lowered to the ground, the red dot no longer flaring in the distance. It's, somehow, by a flash of otherworldly power, been disabled as if one of those cheap spy toys available at pharmacy stores back when I was a child.

"This way," Prisoner 6541a says, pointing to the other end of a little courtyard area, undercut by a thin film of grass that seems much too out of place. I have yet to ask him what the actual plan is, have yet to question where he is taking me. Have yet to ask him the most important question of all—why?

But the man rushes across the grass to an electric gate that crackles like the rest of them, with a blue vengeance, seeking flesh the way a starving man seeks a meal. I stare at the gate, then down at the knife in my hand.

"Tempus," Prisoner 6541a says, as if I should understand what he means by that. I don't.

"Right," I say, remembering what had occurred back at the cell. "Tempus. Should be easy." I raise the knife to the electric gate, then steel my nerves once more. It worked back at the cell. It should work again like a piece of cake after years of eating scraps and dirt.

I slash down with closed eyes, then hear a whirring down as if a system has been turned offline. When my eyes open again, the blue electric gate has vanished, leaving an empty walkway that is almost deceiving under the thin slivers of light that show me a path through.

Prisoner 6541a smiles at me, then walks through the gate. He turns back and rushes me through the adjacent hallway, quickly, and then turns to another hallway where the walls are thick like metal trunks have been erected rather than brick or stone.

It's as if I've turned into another world that shouldn't exist.

"What is this place?" I ask, staring at the vines lit in each corner by thin lights propped along the walls at an even spacing. The vines curl with a naturalness that is so contradictory to the harsh metal glares and slices of alloy bars that characterise much of the prison I call a residence. "What in Old Britain…?"

I've never seen such a place before—or perhaps I have and just don't remember since it was too far back in my memories. This place reminds me of a forest from my childhood, with natural plants flowing across each other, with the wonders of nature and birds and swaying branches providing an ambience so peaceful I would kill for it in the confines of this prison hell.

Along the chunky walls are carvings, right into the stone, thin yet clear to see. Carvings of what looks like times and dates, and scratches of a kind that seems arbitrary, but when looked at closely resemble something of a timeline.

A plan, etched into stone in a corner of the prison that looks unvisited for years and years.

Perhaps this, then, is what Prisoner 6541a brought me here for.

"Now we can talk," Prisoner 6541a says once the electric gate behind us fizzes once more, its crackle an omnipresent reminder of the dangers of the Enclave. But with tempus—or whatever the hell my knife is called—that danger is rendered useless.

I wonder what other secrets Prisoner 6541a has lying in wait for me. What other hidden gems are waiting to be uncovered?

"Talk about what?" I ask, then realise there's a bunch of questions whizzing through my brain, each vying for me to spill them in search for answers. "What is this place?" I decide to ask first. Ease into the questions, then ask the hard-hitting ones a little later on.

"A forgotten place," Prisoner 6541a says. "If you agree to join, then we shall let you know more. This is—shall we say?—part of the prison that is no longer used. Well, officially, anyway."

"Join what?" I say. "You trying to recruit me into something?"

"We are nothing to you if you do not join, Mason," Prisoner 6541a says. His use of my name is pronounced, the 's' sounding more like a snake's hiss than anything else. "We are but mirages in the night, that is all. When you join, *if* you choose to join, then all will be explained. Tempus, the device in my pocket, the strangeness of the prison as of late."

Strangeness? What's he on about? "What kind of strangeness?" I ask.

Prisoner 6541a pulls up the sleeve of his orange shirt and edges closer to me. He lifts it up to the light, and illuminates that scar running from his wrist all the way to the edges of his shoulder. The scar those guards gave when questioning regarding tempus.

"You and I share something," Prisoner 6541a says. "You and I share that we are touched by the same dagger of the Enclave. I wish to extend a hand to you—we can be brothers in arms."

The language isn't exactly cryptic, though it makes the whole thing sound like some sort of club. I've already come all this way with a random man, and my curiosity only runs so deep for me to join some secret organisation—if it can be called that—at the drop of a hat.

But there's something deeper than that curiosity. There's an urge to see through the vision my father had for Old Britain, a vision of destabilising the oppressive dictatorship of the Enclave before they fully seized power and wrecked the entire nation.

Now that they possess that power, my father's vision lives bleakly in my mind, as a far off dream that haunts only the worst of my sleeps. As a reminder of what could've been but never was. As a reminder of something greater than myself that was lost to time and lost possibilities.

But this little excursion out to a forgotten place of the prison, along with the ideas of tempus and whatever other secrets Prisoner 6541a may hold—they all point towards something that aligns with my father's vision.

That glimmer of hope within me threatens to turn into a beacon. If only I will let it.

“What’s the choice, Mason? Ready to come into the light?”

I look to Prisoner 6541a, stare him in the eyes, and my resolve clenches. “I’m ready.”

9

PRISONER 6541A THEN GIVES me a smile once I say the words, the first semblance of human emotion, other than a still stony expression, that I've seen from him since meeting him in Zambol's crazed laboratory. Prisoner 6541a steps closer and embraces me in a hug, his arms wrapping under my shoulders, with the cold of the prison at night being replaced by a warmth I can't describe, yet despite that my entire body freezes.

A memory ruptures my mind in that instant. A distant memory, a memory of something forgotten that now comes back as if a chick returning to the roost of the hen to bathe in its safety and comfort.

The memory is of my mother, with her warm face and bright features, features that filled my child-self with a comfort that never seemed to cease except in her absence. She would pick me up, and then embrace me as if her life depended on it. And I embraced her back too, and felt the love flow between us, its invisible force binding us together. A companionship I haven't felt since that fateful day.

Although the brotherly bond between myself and Prisoner 6541a can never rival that of a mother with her son, the hug almost puts tears in my eyes. As soon as he lets go of me, I quickly wipe my eyes dry and stare at the grey wall with a lot of interest, the warmth still flowing over my body like waves of the ocean in the old summers I haven't experienced in eight years.

"Welcome to the Brotherhood," Prisoner 6541a says. "Your scar is the mark that grants you entry into our group. Tempus, which I shall explain later, is the binding force between us—the thing that puts fear into the heart of the Enclave. After all, any one person questioned on tempus can prove a powerful ally." Prisoner 6541a then taps me on the shoulder, smile still perched in place. "I sincerely hope you can be such an ally within the Brotherhood."

"What…what is this place?" I ask as Prisoner 6541a leads me past the natural-looking greenery and through a massive gap in the stone wall, like a chunk of it has been ripped off by a controlled explosion. "It looks so different."

"It is forgotten, like I mentioned before," Prisoner 6541a says. "Forgotten in the corners of the prison no longer in use. Cells like the ones we stay in once filled these halls. Once the Brotherhood realised the emptiness that lay here, they pounced onto the opportunity in a heartbeat."

I nod, still confused by the entire place, the Brotherhood, and how my life could change in such a short span of time. I feel privy to a secret I shouldn't have access to, roaming freely as if I've stolen a guard's uniform and donned it to fool the Enclave.

The feeling is one of power more than anything. Power as I walk with Prisoner 6541a through a place where the Enclave can't reach, where the tendrils of their influence find a difficulty in entering. My eyes rove all over the stone walls covered with thin strands of ivy that stretch down in natural formations that rival anything artificial that the Enclave can come up with in Zambol's lab.

My hand reaches out, as if it has a mind of its own, and touches the vines. The silky smoothness that meets my fingers almost, rather embarrassingly, makes me swoon. It feels like the nature of Old Britain, like some figment of my childhood has spawned in some forgotten corner of the prison.

"I can assure you, everything is real," Prisoner 6541a says. "There shall be time for exploring later. Time is short, the nights are shorter, especially given recent developments. But for now, what we know is that the Enclave are closing in on finding tempus."

"Which is?" I ask, but Prisoner 6541a shrugs the question off.

"Patience, Mason. I shall answer that once we get inside the mainframe. There is a room here which we use to discuss everything. Someone is there that I wish you to meet."

"Fine," I say, curiosity drumming within me, unsatisfied curiosity. Beside that curiosity is a spindle of hope that grows larger by the second, multiplying like the vines along the wall and thin slits of greenery breaking the stone floor, as if representing the Brotherhood's battle with the Enclave. "Can you tell me your name, at least?"

Prisoner 6541a stops at what seems the entrance to a cave of some sort, where the staggered rock descends to a lower platform, opening to a cavern that stretches far into the darkness. The stone here feels wet to touch, and the thin whir of a fan pulses through the stillness. The first noise I've heard in a while other than our voices.

"My name is Jaxwell," Prisoner 6541a says. "Jaxwell is the only name I have known. I never had a grasp on my surname, and do not now. Does that satisfy you?"

"Nice to meet you Jaxwell," I say, having not spoken those words in years to somebody. A slightly giddy feeling enters me, and then a sliver of worry grows alongside it. Have I been so deprived of proper human interaction that even the slightest bit of normalcy causes me to behave as if gripped by a fever?

Prisoner 6541a—Jaxwell—then carefully climbs down the slippery rock formations, leading me to the lower platform wherein the cavern begins. I almost slip, feet not used to anything except flat surfaces, but a hand grabs my shoulder and rights my body onto the jagged flatness below.

Everything here smells musty, the air wrapped in the heady scent of a warmth I never feel in the freezing conditions of the Enclave Prison at night. The mustiness, akin to the summer forestry near my childhood home, comforts me as Jaxwell leads me over more boulders set into the ground, as if placed there millennia ago to mould with the rest of the rock.

Past everything, in the corner of the cavern's darkest depths, a light blares through the murk like an electric gate firing up or Jaxwell using that device of his that somehow disables cameras. I cover my eyes with a hand, the light almost blinding me for a moment. Then, when the redness fades and the world rights itself again, I let go and stare at what Jaxwell brought me here for.

I haven't seen one in over eight years.

It's a computer—something simple but so complicated for those of us locked here for years. It's not one of the old ones I remember from my childhood, but something more modern. The computer is a massive tower, sleek design glinting and glowing with a neon green light. It flashes once, then twice, and wires extend from it like those vines from earlier. The computer gives way to a massive monitor above it, screen flashing from being booted up, with a loading screen enticing me forwards. I notice a keyboard set like an interactive hologram into the metallic table where the monitor stands, and before that table is a chair.

And a figure sits in that chair, likely the person Jaxwell wanted me to meet.

Jaxwell ventures forward with care after asking me to stay still. "Mason, meet Lizzy. Lizzy, Mason."

Lizzy, evidently the figure in the chair, snaps the seat around and faces me. She's a woman, as I expected, with brown hair mussed almost beyond recognition, like she's trying to join the scraggles of greenery jutting out from the ground behind me. Her eyes are harrowed, as are those of most prisoners within this God-forsaken place. Her face is impossibly thin under the orange prison wear we all don, and those beady eyes inspect me in the same way I'm inspecting her.

"So this is *the* Mason, huh?" Lizzy says. Her voice is scratched, like an owl's caw, and her eyes search me as if a bird watching its prey. Not as friendly as Jaxwell, that's for sure. Her eyes are piercing, as if she has a window into my soul that reveals every intention I have.

I can see why Jaxwell fears her. A shiver races over my spine, too.

Lizzy gets up from her chair, and glares at Jaxwell, before transferring the ire onto me. She stands a little shorter than me, though from this far it's hard to tell.

"I thought we ain't taking in newcomers," Lizzy says. "Never thought the son of the main man himself would ever be 'ere. Bloody fantastic, ain't it?" She whips her gaze to Jaxwell, then returns to me. "Way to get more eyeballs on us, Jax. So much for a 'low profile'."

"He was questioned on tempus," Jaxwell says, as if attempting to plead his case in an Enclave court—which served as nothing except a front for them to punish under the guise of due process. "A worthy allyship could be formed."

"Worthy allyship, yeah? And what about keeping under wraps? Did you think about that Jax, before grabbing the next man and bringing them 'ere?"

"Doesn't the Brotherhood mean—uh—no women," I say, in a tentative tone. Turns out it's the wrong thing to say, as Lizzy's mouth then opens, retort already bubbling in her throat.

"There is history there," Jaxwell says, cutting her off. "Farther back than you can imagine. Let us discuss things at hand first, and then we will explain the history of the Brotherhood."

"Good," I say, "because I have a ton of questions, and I need some answers."

10

As Jaxwell and Lizzy speak to each other in low tones, only bits of which I can catch, I get a better glance around the little cavern that I'm in. Its ceiling is high in some places, barely illuminated rock that slopes down towards the jagged walls as if attempting to enclose the secrets discussed here. I'm growing more familiar in this cavern, since the heady scent transforms into something more homely. As if even a little excursion away from my disastrous cell spells a holiday to enjoy. I can taste a dampness along my tongue—the taste of stale water. But water nonetheless.

I remember reading an old comic as a child—my father brought it back home for me one day, saying he'd found it at an old store where illegal books were sold. Only a few of those stores existed, usually at the back of pubs or behind the censored news section of certain off licences.

It was a comic about a superhero called Batman, written years and years before I was born. Years of torture and prison have deleted the finer details of the story from my mind, but the main theme is still there. A vigilante instilling justice within a corrupt society, all from the bat cave which acted as his headquarters.

This place I'm in now, this forgotten corner of the prison that bleeds into nature, reminds me of the bat cave. Reminds me of that comic from my childhood, and I feel a sense of power enter me, as if I have the strength of Batman. That's what my father wanted, after all, to instil justice within a society that was as corrupt as they came.

And I wish to do the same.

The computer seems more like a hacker's interface than the typical PC I remember from back in the day. The screen flashes multiple times, with lines of code running across the interface as if in a race to the top. I can't understand any of the code-speak written there, though I do interpret files are being accessed.

"What's going on?" I say, noticing that neither Lizzy nor Jaxwell are speaking now. "You wanna answer a few of my questions now?"

"Sure thing," Jaxwell says. "I thought we could get a few of the other members here first, but no matter." He points towards a little drop from the platform, where a table has been erected. It's not a large table, but it blends in with the aesthetic of our little bat cave and holds six chairs around it. "We usually have five of us," Jaxwell says. "The sixth was for Rondon—but he passed a few months ago, as you may remember. It was not exactly underground news."

I do remember—how could I not? That death was as gruesome as they came. Head chopped clean off, right in front of the other prisoners, with minutes of torture beforehand, sadistic and heartless, to prove a point to us and to prolong Rondon's suffering. Of course, we only knew him as a prisoner number I've since forgotten, not his real name.

The Enclave makes sure to dehumanise everyone like that. Strip them of their previous identity in exchange for numbers and tags.

I take a seat in one of the chairs, feeling the comfort of fabric against my backside. Though, considering the cell I stay in and the slave-work I do daily, any form of cushioning, even if made from metal, would give me comfort. Jaxwell, or Jax as I've chosen to call him from now since it's a nickname he doesn't seem to mind, sits to my left. Lizzy comes a few seconds later, clearly still miffed at my being in the Brotherhood, and slumps on a chair to my right. She crosses one leg over the other and stares towards the computer, deliberately not giving me the time of day.

"Firstly," I say, before either of them can jump into another tangent on a topic I have no interest in, "what the heck is the Brotherhood? What is tempus, too? And why the heck have you recruited me of all people?"

"Firstly usually indicates *one* question," Jax says. "But since you asked three, we shall take each one in turn."

"Brotherhood's an old organisation," Lizzy says, and I switch my gaze to her. She still hasn't looked at me, instead speaking to the rock wall in the distance. "Ancient if you ask me. Bloody hounds back in the day decided to tackle the Enclave—don't need to explain who *they* are. Brotherhood were a bunch of people with guts. Bunch of *men* too, which is the story behind the name." Lizzy now does turn to me. "We've still got forces outside this place. Your dad was part of them, the main man himself, though I bet he never told you it was called the Brotherhood, only part of the Uprising movement. That's a rule. No telling anyone not in the organisation."

"Which is a good thing," Jax says. "We cannot have the secrets we learn getting out. Changing—or overthrowing in the case of your father—a government takes diligence and time and knowing when to play your cards."

"Which is why Jax shouldn't have bloody got you in 'ere today," Lizzy says. "So much for strategy. But yeah, we play our cards close to our chest. Only those with a vested interest, as Jax would say, are invited in. And even then we watch closely before to make sure you lot would actually join. No need to get the cat out of the bag early."

I gasp, unable to hold the impulse in. "That's why you gave the knife?" I ask Jax, who nods.

"That is the reason behind the knife. I knew if someone was resourceful enough to hide it from the cameras and the guards, despite an inspection, he would prove resourceful to us. Not to mention who your father is—I am surprised we did not recruit you before. The interrogation over tempus was not in my hands, but proved another reason to get you into the Brotherhood."

"But you could've got me killed," I say, astounded at the shoddy plan Jax was describing. "What if it was another prisoner you gave the knife to and the guards found it? You would've got them handed to the Enclave, and for what? For some weird recruitment thing?"

"Do not fret," Jax says. "I did not have a doubt in your abilities...it was two of the others who thought you would not make a good fit."

"Wait, so you all went behind my back to get this guy?" Lizzy is livid, and even in the dimness the redness of her pale skin shines like the ticker of a bomb about to explode. "You're all gonna have some explaining to do, let me tell you. Bloody embarrassing."

"So what's tempus?" I ask, not wishing to dwell on the domestics of the Brotherhood. Or the fact that my father was a part of this secret organisation without ever telling me. Without even letting a whiff of its existence leave his lips. I bring my knife out of the little pocket in my prison shirt and lay it on the table.

The metal clatters slightly, a sound that echoes through the caverns, and I feel a surge of power along the veins in my hand and wrist. And I have an inkling as to what tempus is.

"Tempus is an element," Jax says. "That is the simplest way to put it. An element like any other metal in the periodic table, which I am sure you learnt since you went to the same school as one of the other members of the Brotherhood."

I wanna know who that is, but Jax decides not to expand and continues along the line of tempus.

"It is a special element, however. Available in few quantities, since there are no deposits, and here is the important detail—"

"The Brotherhood were the ones that found the sucker," Lizzy interrupts, ignoring the frown on Jax's face. "Brotherhood made the discovery, then studied it like proper scientists. Next thing you know, we got a way to fight the Enclave's hyper-electricity, since tempus repels it."

I glance down at the knife whose hilt is wrapped around my palm. "That's why it cuts through the gates?" I ask.

"Got it in one," Lizzy says. "Keep that up and you might not let this whole thing slip to a guard in the next week."

"That's amazing," I say, the potential uses running through my head. I can imagine wars with the guards of the Enclave, battles where they would use their electric guns, tasers, and batons—all utterly useless since we'd have the power of tempus to destroy them. The knife my hand now wraps around, the element it is formed from—it holds a power we can use.

A power that can save the world. "That means we have a chance."

"*Had* a chance," Lizzy says, seemingly unimpressed. "Some Brotherhood people on the outside—you wouldn't know them anyway—are working on getting more tempus out somehow. But this world don't seem to wanna give us anything. Without more of the *actual thing*, how we gonna make enough weapons to fight?"

"We shall find it," Jax says. "That is an inevitability. The deposits we have thus far are enough for a few hundred weapons, but we need thousands, maybe tens of thousands. Time will see it through, I am sure."

"Stop with the poetry," Lizzy says, and I sense a feud between her and Jax stretches back quite far. "We got bigger things to worry about." Lizzy jabs a finger at me. "Like what the hell we're gonna do with new guy here."

"I wanna help," I say, conviction surging alongside my hopes for defeating the Enclave. "That's what I can give the Brotherhood. I…I wanna finish off what my dad started. I wanna save the people of Old Britain."

Jax gives me a sombre look, whilst Lizzy lets off a chuckle.

"You and every other prisoner in this goddamn place," Lizzy says. She leans in, eyes always piercing, calculating. "This ain't some child's game. This is serious stuff. You keep this a secret, and you do your job, and we might just make it out of 'ere. Then, the real fun starts."

"You plan to escape?" I ask. It's an impossible task, though. The prison is fortified beyond anything I've ever seen. There's gates everywhere—

But we have tempus. And tempus can disable the gates. The light Jax has can disable the camera, which could light a path through the prison without being detected—

But the guards are teeming across the perimeter, weapons at the ready. I remember when I was dragged into the prison—the guards had me blindfolded, with a bag over my head. But we walked on concrete, rough like it was starting the punishment before my actual prison stint. The concrete was probably from the courtyard outside the prison, and all I heard was footsteps and talking under low tones. Guards conversing.

Likely hundreds of them guard the perimeters, especially since this is a high-security facility.

There was no chance of escape, hence why I never tried in the last eight years of this hell.

But this whole Brotherhood thing exists right before the noses of the Enclave. An escape isn't off the cards, is it?

"We plan to get *everyone* out at some point," Lizzy says, breaking my spiralling whirl of thoughts. She slaps a hand on the table. The noise echoes. "But that's a dream for another day. We got work to do now, so let's get on with it. Chop chop, no more wasting time."

But it turns out that the work has to be delayed for some time. Perhaps even forever.

Because a noise startles us from the other end of the cavern, in the darkness from which Jax and I entered earlier. A piercing noise from the dark unknown that causes shivers to roam free and hairs to stand on end, as if anticipating a hit.

The noise is the familiar hiss of electricity crackling the murk. And that can only mean one thing.

It's an Enclave guard.

11

WHAT WAS ONCE COMFORTABLE suddenly transforms into a grotesque nightmare right before my eyes. The rock formations, previously comforting in its embrace around the secrets of the Brotherhood, now glint with the metallic sheen of a guard's baton. The electric crackle does nothing to cease, seizing the air with its auditory grip and causing fear to grab us in a similar strangle.

I'm rooted to my chair for a second, that fear causing sweat to perforate my forehead and shivers to perforate my spine. Fear to perforate my heart. I swipe the knife off the table and to my side, the hilt slippery in my clammy fingers.

The darkness, the murk around us, seems to shift and conflate all at once, like it's trying to guide the guard towards where we're hidden. So the guard can kill us for good, ending our sorry existences and destroying the first lease on life I've had in the last eight years.

A surge of conviction, like a second wind, bolsters my resolve, and I stand quietly from the chair. Lizzy and Jax have already stood, and are sending worried glances over towards the whirring computer—where confidential Brotherhood info is stored for convenient access—and the deep from where the guard's electric baton crackle originates.

From where the guard is no doubt about to emerge to hunt us all.

I see a shadow form in the light cast by the computer and its almost holographic screen. The light illuminates a dark clothed body in neon flares, fitted with a torso that features similarly black clothing coloured a tinge of purple. Apt for the murkiness that invades the cave all of a sudden, as if phasing the air to ensnare us all in its grasp.

I shift myself out of the space behind the table, careful not to bump the metal, and slink over to a chunk of rock that sidelines the main upper platform where the guard now stands. The computer is on that platform higher than me, meaning I have the element of surprise if I can wrap around. Jumping up and climbing is a death sentence.

Or, maybe we can hide. Guard realises nothing is here and leaves without another word.

"We ain't letting him see," Lizzy whispers, harshly. She's lucky, since a crackle of the guard's baton masks her voice and its echo. I see her grab something from her pocket—a shiv, hopefully imbued with tempus.

I stiffly grip my own knife, then lean into the sliminess of the rock. I feel some of it crumble and hit the ground, and my foot almost slips on the crumbs of dust. A glance back reveals Lizzy near the table, ducking under it and using the glinting metal as cover, weapon in hand. Jax is nowhere to be seen, having retreated to the shadows where the guard, nor us, can detect him.

He's a planner, a schemer. I only hope that what he's planning reaches us in time.

"What's this?" the guard says, his voice gravelly as always yet barely above a whisper. His baton crackles as if excited at the discovery of the computer. Discovery of information on tempus, no doubt, since only the Brotherhood knows what it is.

Lizzy's right. That information can't get out. If it does, our entire mission, to save Old Britain, is done for. And my new grip on life will have been short-lived, and for nothing.

I shift along the face of the rock wall, keeping my body close to the ridges and sharp edges. All the while my knife sits in my loose hand like an idle fiend waiting to be unleashed. The stone, jagged like it had been slit with geometric intention, digs into my shoulders, and I hear a whir again from the computer.

"This is...." But the guard must be too shocked for words. Has he discovered what tempus is? I hear shuffling as I reach the other end of the little path I'm traversing, the darkness masking my movements, my breathing as light as possible to hide my presence.

The guard then stops talking, and his baton again crackles. That means he's activated it. He knows someone is here, knows someone is in the deep darkness of the caverns. The computer was left unlocked, and the guard knows that means someone's nearby.

He even says as much.

"You're dead, you hear me." That corporate evil in the typical guard's voice gives way to a harsh hammer of a tone. "You either die a slow death or a fast one. Come out now or face the Enclave's worst. You're the one that decides."

But, for obvious reasons, neither Lizzy nor Jax speak out. I concentrate on light footsteps along the crumbling rock, along the dirt that scrapes under my bare feet like thickets of quicksand attempting to stall me.

"You hear me?" the guard then shouts. The echo bashes into my back as I scale the slightly uphill path towards the upper platform, hand on the wall for balance and to keep noise at a minimum. I'm almost there, almost at the flat patch of cave leading to the upper platform where the computer resides.

Where the other two are—Lizzy and Jax—I haven't a clue.

Have they retreated, leaving me here to deal with the guard on my own? They don't strike me as the cowardly types, though one can never tell.

Another crack of electricity pierces the temporary silence, and shivers race over my skin. As if my body is reacting in anticipation of being shocked once more. The scar on my arm, running to my shoulder, pulses as I reach the upper platform.

A heat presses into my skin, sweat pouring down like the stormy rainwater I haven't seen in over eight years.

I peek over the top of the rock face and find the guard staring at the computer, then turning to face the darkness on the other side of the cavern where the table is located. If I can get behind him, I can skewer him with the knife. Surely the Enclave won't notice one dead guard, right? There's thousands in this place.

Then a bang erupts on the other side of the cavern, rupturing the musty air with a tension that clings like desperate dust. And immediately my body shivers and slips against the rock, snapping noise into the quiet.

Crap. Crap crap crap.

What the heck made that bang?

I don't have time to think. Time to breathe. Time to survive.

And I don't need to hear the grunt from the guard, nor the crackle of his electric baton. All I need to see is the looming shadow against the wall, like a demon at night, or those shifting forms when sleep paralysis takes hold. That shadow against the wall enlarges, its fuzzy edges growing sharper by the millisecond. My fear follows suit, and my grip on the knife almost topples.

I slide down the side of the rock, the soles of my feet feeling clammy against the clumps of dirt threatening to pull me under. Like they're digging an early grave for me. Like they know my fate and are accelerating the inevitable.

I intake a harsh breath, a gasp that creates a tense silence that bubbles in my being. I hold that breath despite my lungs begging to breathe.

The shadow looms larger. Grows like Zambol's chemicals malfunctioning. Grows like the swollen muscles of a prisoner being electrocuted beyond recognition.

I hold the knife, tighten my grip around it to almost the point of destroying my knuckles, and then the guard's black uniform and red mask turn the corner. I'm backsliding, and he spots me easily in the murk.

"There you are," he says, eyes widening beneath the mask. "You're one of the ones in this little place, aren't you? Sneaky sleepwalking little—"

"Now," Lizzy shouts in the distance from somewhere in the darkness behind me.

A bright, brilliant flash of blue light illuminates the cavern as if the crackling electricity has suddenly painted the entirety of everyone's vision. I stumble backwards, blinded as my eyes clamp shut, for a second seized by seismic shocks to my eyelids. It's all tinged with a blue film, and my back smacks into a wall. My head snaps back, and stars line my vision.

The knife drops from my hand.

Sense smacks into me once more.

Crap crap crap.

I scramble to my knees, eyes open again, aware of the guard merely seconds from reaching me. My hands scrape the dirt, desperation clawing at my limbs as I struggle to stay in control. A footstep roars from where I'd stumbled back from, and my vision clears the blue halo as my fingers wrap around the tip of the knife.

A crackle snatches the world to my left, so I grab what tentative hold I have of the knife and throw myself to the right. The hint of a shock hits me, right as my shoulder hits the metal table, and a chair crashes to the ground.

I sit up, swing the knife around so its hilt sits in my palm, and scramble to my feet. The chair is trodden behind me, another potential weapon just in case.

The guard looks down at me, easily a foot taller, and his eyes are narrowed beneath the red mask. His eyes flare like what I imagine are the devil's eyes, instilled with an evil that those like me can't even comprehend, only witness the effects of.

The guard slaps the baton in his other hand, as if readying it for maximum damage.

"So there's more than one of you?" he says, letting the baton fizz in his fingers. "That's all right. More ditches for the prison undertakers to dig. You want to play with your life, go ahead. None escape the Enclave." He sweeps his gaze fearlessly across the darkness, inspecting for where Lizzy went, since she shouted, and where Jax, since he caused the flash of light, hides. He chuckles, once, then points the baton down at me, evil staining every feature in sight. "None can escape the Enclave. Especially not *you*, Mason Sharp."

I steady the knife, right as his baton crackles, and the electricity sends its first shocks of attack.

12

THE BATON SWIPES TOWARDS me, the guard sending it with a force that fields immense anger behind it, as if every fibre in his body, let alone the charged hyper-electricity, wants me dead as a corpse. The baton arcs through the air, right as my knife rises in response, the hilt clamping in my fingers, and smacks the baton head on.

The impact shoots me back, the forces colliding as if planetary bodies smashing into one another. The clatter of metal rings my eardrums like rattling prison bars, as I stumble back and find my footing just before the fallen chair.

A faint shock runs through me from the baton hit, akin to a small tinge of electricity racing across the jittering nerves. But it's nothing compared to what usually grips me upon a baton's shock. The usual pain, agony, and instant submission to whoever is doing the shocking.

The cavern, almost impossibly, immediately brightens, darkness retreating to allow the light to wash the cavern walls with a sense of hope. That hope expands the scope of possibilities, and my grip on the knife strengthens. That power I first felt when holding the knife now courses through me, far stronger than a mere electric tap.

Tempus works. It actually bloody works.

I glance at the knife I hold, wondering whether I can really win, for the first time, against an Enclave guard.

The guard doesn't want me to, however, then makes that known with another smack of the baton. This time, I snap my legs to the right, dangerously close to a side-face of ridged rock. I swing the knife down just as the baton comes, and the two connect once more.

The knife is almost knocked from my hand, but the electricity doesn't faze me. I feel no shiver, no shock, and an immense power surges through me in its absence. The cave brightens even more, and it's as if I can see light again for the first time.

"What's happening?" the guard says, looking at his baton. "You bloody done something, haven't you?"

I don't respond, because this time I'm on the offensive. I rush forwards, arms feeling a strength I haven't felt since running through woods as a child free from prison, and slam the knife down.

The guard barely has time to activate the baton, but its electricity does nothing. The baton swings out from his hand when I strike it, and he falls back. His back smacks the rock wall, and he groans from the impact.

I'm immediately onto him. I slam him with a shoulder back into the wall when he tries to get up, and stars line my own vision as if transferred from him. He gives a grunt as I dig the knife into him, but the guard armour he wears protects it from piercing skin. Protects it from causing his death.

An immense anger washes over me. Anger from years of being tortured, years of facing persecution at the hands of guards like these. Years of having my backside handed to me. Years of electricity fizzing through every pore of my body.

And now I have a real chance at revenge—I'm taking it with every ounce of energy I have.

Tempus forgotten, I chuck the knife to the side and grab the guard's neck with both hands. A rage fuels me, ignites my body and my mind with a fury that seems all-encompassing. I don't stop to think for even a second, just dig my fingers around the guard's pudgy neck and stare into his evil eyes that widen with every second strangled.

And in those eyes I see fear. The first signs of fear behind that blood red mask from an Enclave guard in eight years.

I hear shuffling behind me. Probably Lizzy and Jax, but those two are the farthest from my mind. All I can think about, all I'm consumed by, is the roaring strength flowing through my veins and that sole mission of revenge.

The world dims around me, as if mimicking the light within the guard's eyes. He's squirming, and my grip wanes as the malnutrition and tiredness finally takes hold of the adrenaline and chucks it to the side. My muscles are starting to weaken, and the thin slices of panic begin to set in.

But he needs to die. Needs to pay for the crimes he's committed over the years. Needs to pay for the role he played in my father's death as a guard, in the death of so many people at the hands of the Enclave.

But my grip is slipping, clammy fingers struggling for control, and clammy feet crumbling in the dirt.

And then my grip slips entirely.

The guard coughs immediately, then pushes me away. I trip over a loose rock and tumble down. Now I'm the one on my back, head near-missing the boulder to my left, and the guard is on his feet again.

He doesn't need the baton. A taser now sits in his hand, pulled from the back of a belt he wears, a taser imbued with a hyper-electricity that can kill.

I feel around for my tempus knife, but the thing is gone, no longer in the pocket of my prison clothes. In my rage, I chucked the knife to the side. And now I'm at the mercy of the guard. A guard who has no mercy.

And he wastes no time in getting back at me.

He rushes towards me, taser at the ready, and I revert to old patterns. My eyes close, the crackle of electricity filling my ears like gongs going off, and wait for the shock to race over my skin.

But a shout comes instead. My eyes flash open.

Lizzy smacks the taser out of the guard's hand with her tempus shiv, disabling the electricity, then slams his skull against a rock. Jax joins from the other side and blasts that blue light device, filling the cavern with illumination.

I close my eyes, breathing hard whilst lying on the dirt, flash-banged with the scores of blue. Once the light fades, my eyes open, and the guard is still, unmoving. Slumped against the wall, and Lizzy leans off him.

Her shiv holds blood from the guard's neck. The guard's blood—he's dead. She's taken his life, and he's a threat no longer. I've seen deaths before, but this one seems as if the first time. The rage within me subsides, and a sliver of self-loathing enters.

How could I let myself lose control like that? If I hadn't been so hell-bent on revenge after the last eight years, I wouldn't have thrown my knife to the ground. I would've actually fought properly, and won like Lizzy, and achieved what that anger had been striving for in the first place—finally winning against a guard that wants me dead.

Lizzy glances down at me, wiping her shiv against the boulder besides me. "You got the passion for this, I'll tell you that. But you ain't got the strength to kill someone, not a guard anyway. Not yet."

I don't know what to think of her words, so I look to Jax. He's by the computer, staring at the screen to check something, so

I instead wash my gaze over the cavern as normal breathing returns to my exhausted body.

The cave darkens a little as the battle with the guard ends. Everything returns to normal. Pockets of darkness in corners of the cave my vision can't pierce, mixed with boulders illuminated by slants of light that come from the computer screen and LED keyboard.

I sigh, the musty air streaming into my lungs and filling it with used oxygen that is nasty to breathe but a relief since I'm still alive after fighting with an Enclave guard.

"You okay, though?" Lizzy says, grasping my attention. "Fight like that ain't the best thing on your first day."

Embarrassment washes through me. "I'm all right, and thanks for the save."

I sit up, then stand, then look away from her and grab my knife from where I'd chucked it earlier. I stare at the sharp edge of the tempus blade, and remember once more how I threw it away in the throes of rage. A throw that could've cost my life.

"You need to stay calm, Mason," Jax says. "We have…rather unfortunately…been on the receiving end of numerous fights. Not only guards over the last five years, but even a few prisoners have decided to take their anger out on us for whatever reason they come up with." Jax walks over and claps me on the shoulder. "You must stay in control, and avoid fighting whenever possible, understand?"

I nod, recalling how Lizzy and Jax hid and bided their time whilst I immediately went for the jugular, to put it bluntly.

"Brotherhood ain't about getting dirty," Lizzy says. "We work from the shadows, and we wanna keep it that way." She sticks a finger in my direction, then talks to Jax. "You sure he don't have anything to do with why that guy found us?"

"Maybe we left a trail somewhere," Jax says, rubbing his chin. "Enclave won't suspect a thing, and if we bury the body further down the cave, the bugs and bacteria will come feed on it and get rid of the evidence." Jax sighs, steps down from the platform where the computer is, and we're all standing around the table once more. The smell of blood fills the air, and I can't mask it out. "Mason is not at fault, though. No one would deliberately bring a guard here only to almost die themselves. I think we *did* leave a trace somewhere."

"But why's the guard even 'ere like this?" Lizzy says. She rests a hand on the table, her shiv in the other. It's still dripping dark blood. I glance over at the guard. A hole resides in his neck. "Don't make any sense, you feel me? Guards ain't even supposed to be 'ere at night, since no prisoner can get out. How on earth…?"

"It's a mystery," I say. Then I remember a crucial detail that flashes back now the tension has largely sifted out of my body. "I think he might have it out for me, though. I think it's something personal, but I don't know what."

"You ain't that special," Lizzy says with a laugh. "Just cos of who your dad is."

"It's not that. Did you notice how he said my name, not prisoner number?"

Jax's eyes widen, since he knows the implications. "Are you sure he said your name?"

"Said it loud and clear," Lizzy says with a nod, eyes flashing with recognition. "Heard it with my own ears. Means he has something against you. Means he planned to come 'ere. Damn…."

Lizzy rushes up the path to the upper platform and taps a few keys at the computer. "He knows your name—guards ain't supposed to—and then he comes in 'ere and tries to kill you? Something's up, and we need to find what it is."

"Perhaps they are catching wind of the Brotherhood?" Jax says, chin still being rubbed. "That cannot be possible now, since I disabled the camera attached to his uniform with the Bright device. But still, it does beg the question as to how much they know of us."

"We need to stay careful, then," I say.

"You more than anyone, definitely," Jax says. "If the man has—*had*—a vendetta against you, then surely there will be more like-minded as him. And maybe this is symptomatic of a larger problem. I shall inform the other members in due course, take the guard's weapons and dispose of them, and you might want to sleep since the night only has a few hours left. Oh, and clean up using these wipes here. Your feet can't have dirt, and evidence of fighting is anything but good."

Jax hands me the wipes Lizzy picks out from a drawer underneath the computer. The wipes are made from the softest material I have ever touched, and I promptly clean myself of the thin stains of red attached to my orange clothing. The stains disappear almost instantly, and I wonder what other technology the Brotherhood has access to. I finish wiping the rest of my exposed skin, cleaning most of the grime.

Jax then spreads his arms around the cave, then signals to the computer blaring its neon screen from where Lizzy sits. "We have much work to do, it seems, and not enough time to do it."

"We're gonna save Old Britain, right?" I say, for some reason needing to hear it from them, as some kind of confirmation before this bizarre night, the most bizarre in all my life, is over. "All of us, and the Brotherhood outside the prison—we're gonna save everyone?"

"That's the goal ain't it, Mason?" Lizzy drawls. "Whole reason we're doing this, so don't ask dumb questions again."

Jax gives me a smile, a small gesture, but it feels golden amongst the brown and black dumps of dirt that surround us in this dingy yet hope-filled cave.

"Lizzy shall clean this all up, not to worry. Let me take you back to your cell. And yes, Mason, we *will* save Old Britain. And the people shall sing once more."

13

THE WALK BACK TO the cell is uneventful, and this time the confusion that wrought me on the way to the Brotherhood's secret hideout vanishes. I have a purpose now, a reason to exist, a reason to battle through the pain that the Enclave are determined to strike me with.

The natural vines and stone that characterise the hall leading to the Brotherhood's bat cave separate it from the rest of the prison. Like a haven away from the horrors we must endure every day. Hunger wracks my body every second since the last meal was hours before, but determination causes my hunger's grip to wane.

I have a purpose now, and that purpose rings around my head like my thoughts are a pin machine as the grey, bland hallways lead us into the main prison once more. The silence, once frightening and eerie, now bubbles around me like some apparition of the hope that resides in my heart.

As Jax said, we will free Old Britain from the destructive grasp of the Enclave. We have that power—the power of tempus, of a way to fight back—and we will use it to save the people being oppressed and fulfil the mission my father had set out for all those years ago.

I can taste the hope on my tongue, and it spreads the sweetness of sugary buns from my childhood, the ones my mother used to buy as treats once a month. The only treats that month.

But when we liberate the country from the oppressive strangle of the Enclave, those treats will be available always. And it's a mission I wanna see through to the end.

I slash through any electric gates with a strength that wasn't there a few hours ago, and Jax flashes cameras with his device so they disable and don't see us. Jax hasn't explained why that occurs, and how the Enclave do not realise the cameras are down, but I'm sure he will, in time.

Jax leads me to my cell, then quickly flashes the camera within to stop it from seeing me. I hack through the electric gate with my tempus knife, no longer scared of it spasming my body, and step into the cell. The cold hits me right away, and the chills arrive, but they no longer scare me. I've turned, almost, fearless.

"Onto a new beginning," Jax says.

I turn and give a smile—the first in what seems like years. "Stop with the poetry."

Jax chuckles, then pockets his Bright device and walks away to wherever his cell is amongst the gallows that thread through the Enclave's prison. I grip the knife stashed in the pocket of my prison clothes. I need to find a new hiding spot for it, since guards will search my cell soon, and I can't take it with me to any slave-work without immediately being caught.

If the guards find it, the mystery of tempus is already over. And I need a way to fight their electricity if I'm to win this battle.

For now, I lie back in my bed and place the knife into the seam of the mattress. There's another three days till the next inspection, at least at my estimates, meaning I have some time to sort that out.

The mattress isn't comfortable—digs into my back and feels like I've got stalagmites rupturing my spine. I remember my dad once, in the winter, taking me into the mouth of a cave with such large stalagmites and stalactites, as he called them. He was a staunch believer in God, though I'm less so, and told me to ponder over how beautiful nature is. Though I'm not as certain as to the creator of nature, I agree that it gives off a spiritual sense of peace that cannot be totally described, only pored into.

As the darkness ebbs and flows around me, no longer the terrifying murk I was used to each night, that memory floats to my mind. The chill within the prison is forgotten for the cold of that winter with my father—I was fifteen at the time, and had no idea that the next two years would bring the downfall of everything I loved.

The cave was beautiful, situated right at the roof of the mountainous region close to where we lived. At that time, the Enclave didn't allow any personal vehicles to be driven, only state-sanctioned public transport, one of the earliest encroachments on our freedom that they enforced.

But my father was a determined man if nothing else, so packed our bags and walked with me the ten mile hike required to reach that cave.

That day presented a beautiful shade of white in the sky, with tickles of snow falling down as if visitors welcoming us up the steep paths and narrow valleys. The trees were caked in layers of white like those powdery pastries my mother told stories about from her own childhood. The breeze brought with it cold, but every breath felt fresher than the one before, like we were in some mystical heaven.

I remember glancing to the sky and wishing we could be as free as we were then. In the remoteness of the hills, at least at that time, there was no Enclave to spy on us, no drones passing overhead with their intrusive buzzing and constant surveillance. No officers banging on the door in the middle of the night for some requested questioning that, if refused, could lead to a prison sentence.

Only the openness of Old Britain and the delights that it brought. An openness that, even in that remote place, would soon be stripped away.

We climbed to the summit of one particular hill, and my father promptly sat on a boulder after hauling himself up. Legs dangling, he swung his bag around and grabbed a sandwich. Handed it to me, and then grabbed one for himself. We ate quietly outside the mouth of that cave, and once we finished my father stood up.

"Onwards, Mason," he said. "Come with me."

The relationship between a good father and his son is one of trust, and I trusted him fully then. He stepped into the mouth of the cave, suspended himself into the darkness, the unknown, and I followed him without another thought.

When he grabbed a torch—a device that was banned a year later as it could 'endanger' animals, the Enclave's idea of an excuse—and lit the cave up, I saw an infusion of blue light that truly astounded me.

"Temperatures up here are always freezing year round," my father explained. He pointed to the spikes hanging upside down from the ceiling, as if teeth about to chomp on the ice below for a quick snack. "Stalagmites and stalactites. My own father brought me here, Mason, and told me what I'm about to tell you."

I shivered, but not from the cold. I shivered from the sense that a moment of great gravity was about to pass, a moment that would imprint itself upon me for years to come. "What's that?" I remember asking.

"You see this freedom here, in this cave—our people don't have that in the rest of Britain. And it's up to us, our God-given mission, to get rid of this bloody Enclave once and for all." His grey gaze pierced me. "You understand?"

A son always looks up to his father, always trusts him fully, especially in his early teenage years. I nodded without a second thought, his mission then fusing with mine.

"If I fail, I want you to be my successor. You understand?"

I nodded once again. We thereafter exited the cave, sat on that boulder and ate another round of sandwiches, before trekking all the way down the mountain and back home.

I didn't uphold his mission, however. After his death, I felt as if my whole life fell apart, and since I was in such a state, the Enclave made up a psychological diagnosis to suggest I couldn't be trusted in society. And then they locked me up for life, like many of the other Uprising supporters here. Locked with no sense of return to the ways of Old, before the tyrants won.

But this Brotherhood has given a revival to that mission dormant within my heart. A mission stamped on by the Enclave, forced to the recesses of my mind as some far off dream never to be accomplished.

Even though there'll be dangers, attempts on my life, more torture and suffering, and perhaps even death—I know my father's mission, descended to be my own, is the most important thing.

I'll stand against the Enclave, and stand firm for the people of Old Britain. A second Uprising, if that's what it takes.

And as I lie in a prison cell now, with nothing but the prison clothes on my back, the Brotherhood, and a singular tempus knife—the determination through my veins has never been so strong.

Newsletter

FOR WRITING UPDATES AND info on new releases, sign up to our newsletter!

About MFP

The Muslim Fiction Project, MFP, is an initiative started by S. H. Miah to publish works of fiction that promote Islamic messages for Muslims all around the world.

Written for Muslims. By a Muslim.

Visit our website to see what other stories you could sink your teeth into!

About S. H. Miah

S. H. Miah is the founder of Muslim Fiction Project. An initiative to produce high-quality Muslim fiction. Written for Muslims. By a Muslim.

When not writing, S. H. Miah enjoys spending time with family and friends, charging through his own reading list, and of course having a bit too large an obsession with spiral-bound notebooks.

For more information about Muslim Fiction Project, please visit: https://www.muslimfictionproject.com